*To every hopeless romantic:*
*May you find true love in unexpected places.*

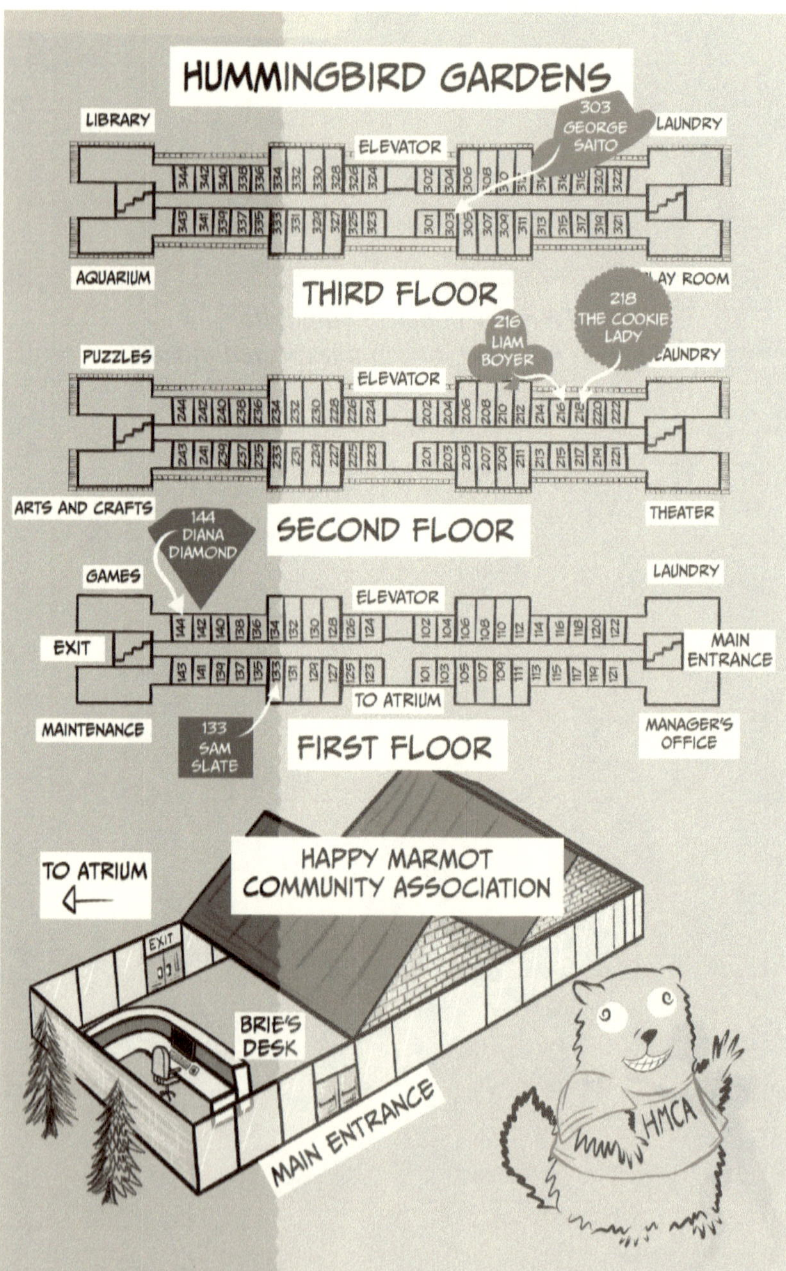

HUMMINGBIRD GARDENS

LIBRARY
303
GEORGE
SAITO
LAUNDRY

ELEVATOR
344 342 340 338 336 334 332 330 328 326 324 302 304 306 308 310 312 314 316 318 320 322
343 341 339 337 335 333 331 329 327 325 323 301 303 305 307 309 311 313 315 317 319 321

AQUARIUM
THIRD FLOOR
PLAY ROOM

218
THE COOKIE
LADY

216
LIAM
BOYER

PUZZLES
LAUNDRY

ELEVATOR
244 242 240 238 236 234 232 230 228 226 224 202 204 206 208 210 212 214 216 218 220 222
243 241 239 237 235 233 231 229 227 225 223 201 203 205 207 209 211 213 215 217 219 221

ARTS AND CRAFTS
SECOND FLOOR
THEATER

144
DIANA
DIAMOND

GAMES
LAUNDRY

ELEVATOR
144 142 140 138 136 134 132 130 128 126 124 102 104 106 108 110 112 114 116 118 120 122
EXIT
143 141 139 137 135 133 131 129 127 125 123 101 103 105 107 109 111 113 115 117 119 121
MAIN
ENTRANCE

TO ATRIUM

MAINTENANCE
133
SAM
SLATE
FIRST FLOOR
MANAGER'S
OFFICE

TO ATRIUM

HAPPY MARMOT
COMMUNITY ASSOCIATION

EXIT

BRIE'S
DESK

MAIN ENTRANCE

HMCA

# Grandma's Valentine Abduction

Also by the mother-daughter writing team
Catherine Dilts and Merida Bass

The Ninja Grandparent Placement Mysteries:

Grandpa's New Year's Relocation

YA Sci-fi writing as Ann Belice

The Tapestry Tales:

Frayed Dreams

Broken Strands

Also by Catherine Dilts

Survive or Die

The Rock Shop Mysteries:

Stone Cold Dead

Stone Cold Case

Stone Cold Blooded

The Rose Creek Mysteries:

The Body in the Cattails

The Body in the Cornfield

The Body in the Hayloft

Children's books by Merida Bass

The Apple of My Eye, written and illustrated by Merida Bass

The Jelly Monster, written by C.S. Gieck, illustrated by Merida Bass

# Grandma's Valentine Abduction

**The Ninja Grandparent Placement Mysteries**
**Book Two**

## Catherine Dilts * Merida Bass

Author photo by Winston Foto at https://www.winstonfoto.com

Paperback ISBN 978-1-967578-17-7
E-book ISBN 978-1-967578-18-4
LCCN 2026900538

First Edition: February 2026

Published by Top Hat Cat Publishing LLC

https://merida-creates.com/

Printed in the United States of America

10 9 8 7 6 5 4 3 2 1

Top Hat Cat

Publishing LLC

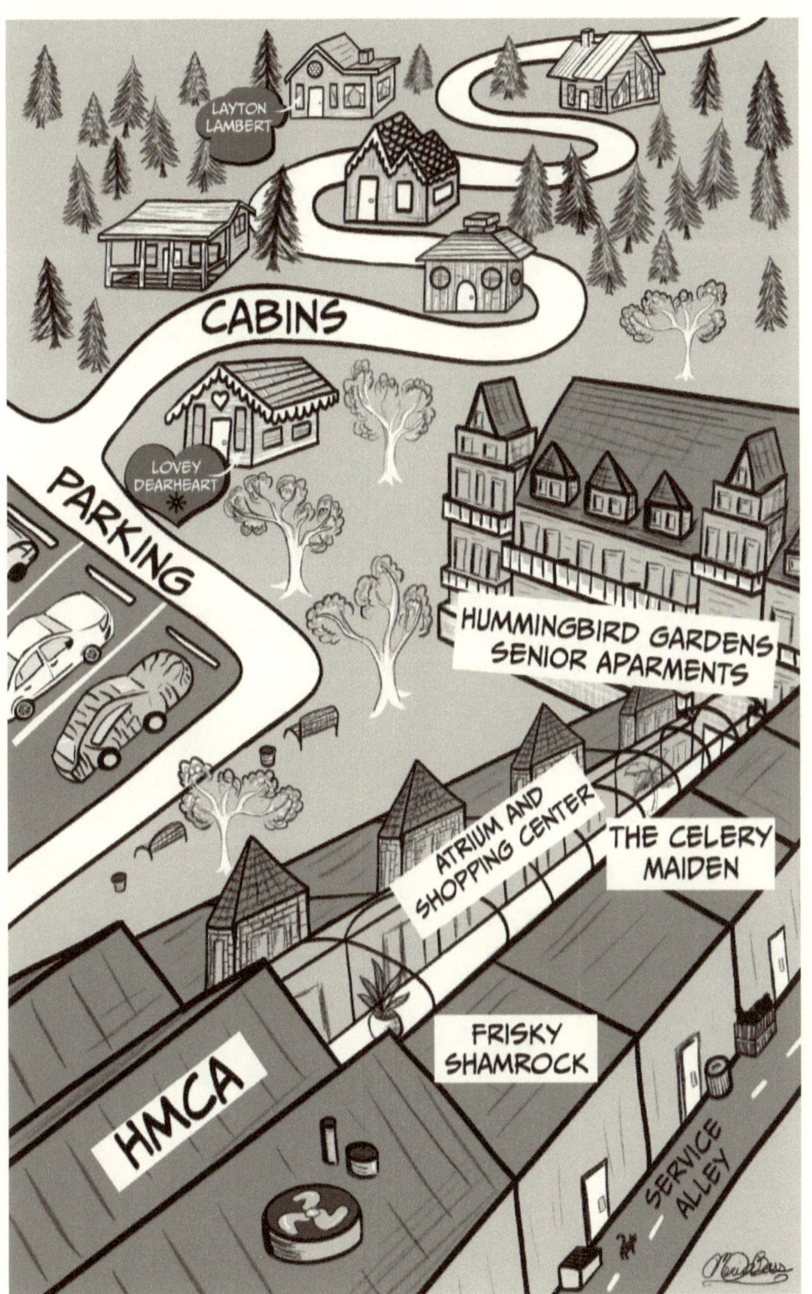

LAYTON LAMBERT
CABINS
LOVEY DEARHEART
PARKING
HUMMINGBIRD GARDENS SENIOR APARMENTS
ATRIUM AND SHOPPING CENTER
THE CELERY MAIDEN
FRISKY SHAMROCK
HMCA
SERVICE ALLEY

# 1

## ✳ Lovey ✳

Lovey Dearheart cuddled her miniature poodle.

"Let's get ready for dance class, Duchess."

"Yip!" Duchess kissed Lovey's chin with her pink tongue.

After a quick hug, Lovey set her precious pup on the sofa. The little dog was pink from her fluffy ears to her puffball tail. The tags dangling from her shiny red collar tinkled as Duchess paced in circles on the couch.

"We can't go out in public without accessories," Lovey said. She attached a red rosette decoration with silver sparkles to Duchess's collar. As a former Las Vegas showgirl, Lovey had a keen sense of fashion. "There. Now let's bundle up!"

Lovey pulled on her faux fur coat, a fun, poofy fuchsia affair with a matching hat and gloves. She slid her feet into pink snow boots with magenta pompoms. Lovey slipped a matching coat onto Duchess, carefully strapping on the tiny snow boots. The pup was well behaved, so Duchess rarely had to endure the indignity of a leash. Most of the time, Duchess was cradled in Lovey's arms.

Picking up her designer tote bag full of feather boas and ostrich plume fans, she opened the door of her cottage to a winter wonderland. After Duchess was safely on the front doormat, Lovey pulled the door closed. She double checked to make sure it was locked. The Gardens staff reminded their senior tenants that it was easy to forget security in such an idyllic living situation. The doggy door was perpetually unclasped, but no human could fit through the tiny square opening.

A February storm had dumped several inches of snow on the city of Colorado Springs. The Hummingbird Gardens Senior Apartments' groundskeepers did an excellent job clearing the sidewalks connecting the cottages to the rest of the property.

She didn't mind days like this, when her short walk to the Happy Marmot Community Association would be crisp. But she felt sorry for poor Duchess, prancing in her designer boots across a sidewalk crunchy with snowmelt pellets.

The HMCA classes Lovey taught brought in a little extra money, which was important when one lived on a fixed income. They also gave her the chance to keep shining on small, local stages, while encouraging her peers to stay active. At sixty-nine, she made it her mission to maintain her own fitness and style.

"Keep dancing to stay sexy!" was her class motto.

Her cottage at Hummingbird Gardens didn't come cheap, but it was worth every penny. She blended in here, as much as that was possible for someone as recognizable as Lovey. Her time back in the '90s hosting the cable TV show, *The Hopeless Romantic*, didn't make her *that* famous, and yet obsessive fans did make life uncomfortable at times.

Despite her flashy personality, Lovey guarded her privacy like a sacred treasure.

A blast of wind-driven snow assaulted Lovey from behind. She shivered and pulled the hood of her furry coat up to protect her carefully coiffed silver hair. Drifts scuttled across the sidewalk. She bent down to pick up Duchess, afraid the little pup would blow away.

"Yip!" Duchess licked Lovey's gloved fingers. Then she wriggled and pulled away.

"You still want to walk, in this weather?"

"Yip!"

Lovey set Duchess down, and the little dog darted up the sidewalk. Lovey wasn't concerned. If Duchess got too far ahead, she would either run back to find Lovey or wait for her at the Happy Marmot Community Association building.

If it weren't for Lovey's devoted class requesting an emergency session on a Sunday afternoon, she would be tempted to turn back to her cottage. But it was such a short walk. Despite the reliance of some of the seniors on canes or walkers, they were determined to perform in the Valentine's Showcase. Her students had heart, but they needed more practice. And they only had seven days to get ready for the show.

Lovey had very few close friends and no family, other than Duchess. She had focused on her career, and then had been unlucky in her choices in male companionship. One day, she realized it was too late for a family of her own. The Hummingbird Gardens community was her lifeline.

Lovey couldn't disappoint her students.

Duchess shivered in the distance, waiting in front of the doors to the atrium that connected the senior apartments to the HMCA. Heavy flakes dropped a white veil over the scene and coated her puppy's pink winter coat like icing on a cupcake. *A pupcake!*

The sound of wind whistling through the evergreens pulled Lovey out of her musings. She steadied herself against a gust that painted her vision white with snow. Duchess disappeared from view. Lovey's breath caught in her chest. Had the little dog actually blown away? For a moment, Lovey considered the practicality of a leash for times like these.

*Don't panic.* The last she saw Duchess, the pup was safe. *She has to be okay. She's all I have.*

"If only I had been luckier in love," Lovey said quietly, trusting her dog's super hearing to catch her words. "I'd have a human family to watch you on a day like this."

Even though Duchess had stolen Lovey's very heart and soul, she sighed, pondering the choices that had led her to this solitary life.

"I wish I had a family."

Without warning, the snow ramped up to blizzard intensity. A whirlwind twisted violently through the pine trees. She pressed on, tightening her hood, careful not to smudge her lipstick. Lovey would be a diva to her dying day. Much like her beloved canine companion Duchess, Lovey might look like a delicate confection. In reality, she could handle tough situations.

She felt confident she could take care of herself until she stepped down with one boot, right onto a patch of hidden ice. Her foot slipped. Lovey threw her arms out, struggling to maintain her balance.

A hand grasped her arm, firm through the thick cushioning of the fuchsia faux fur.

"Thank you," Lovey said. "I was afraid I was headed for a bad fall—"

She tried to look around at her savior, but a black hood dropped over her head, muffling her vision.

"Stop! Help!"

Lovey had no choice but to fight, despite the risk to her manicure. She balled her hands into fists, although her gloves would soften any blows she managed to land. Swinging frantically, she caught only air.

Had the obsessed fan flooding Lovey's mailbox with letters crossed a line and gone full-blown stalker? The fame being a cable TV star brought her shouldn't be enough to warrant this level of frightening attention.

*I have to fight! Duchess needs me!*

Lovey kicked out with her boots. In her day, she had fought off the unwelcome advances of thugs much larger than the person currently attempting to ensnare her. In fact, the slight form her gloved hands groped for was not much larger than her own five-foot, hundred-pound soaking wet physique.

*A woman?*

Lovey struggled to keep her feet under her, but her boots

skidded and slipped on the walkway. Groping fingers prodded Lovey's neck despite her hood. She felt a pinch.

"Who are you?" Lovey gasped.

"I'm going to assure you receive the most love you've ever had on Valentine's Day," a distorted female voice said.

And then, the world went dark.

# 2

# ❋ Brie ❋

A cacophony of shuffling feet, squeaky wheels, and clattering canes drew Brie Bramble's attention away from her work computer. She was surprised to see an entire herd of gym patrons from the Hummingbird Gardens Senior Apartments converging on her desk.

Sundays at the HMCA were extra busy this time of year. Patrons were still dedicated to New Year's resolutions they'd made last month. Brie didn't mind working weekends at the Happy Marmot Community Center. Unlike most people in their mid-twenties, she didn't have much of a social life.

Brie paused her true crime podcast and tugged the earbud from her ear. Before she could greet the seniors, they launched into distressed clamoring. Brie raised her hands.

"Please. One at a time. What's going on?"

"Where is Lovey?" Diana Diamond asked. Her concern was emphasized with the stern look in her brown eyes. The woman was in her mid-sixties, but her smooth dark skin barely creased with her frown.

"Lovey told us she would meet up with us this afternoon." Layton Lambert tugged at the sparkling black sweatband stretched across his brown forehead, lifting it against his graying brown curls. The faint scent of saffron wafted from the gourmand. The big man had the look of a person who had been lean and fit, once upon a time. Maybe like a college track star gone to seed. "She's ten minutes late! We planned an emergency practice session."

"An emergency?" Brie scrunched her nose. *What kind of emergency requires proper feather boa etiquette?* Brie had observed the class through the wall of glass that made up one side of the seniors' classroom. It was labeled a jazz dance class in the HMCA system, but Brie was pretty sure what Lovey taught was actually a family-friendly version of burlesque.

"We're putting on a show in seven days," Diana explained. "We're part of the Valentine's Showcase."

Brie had been grateful she wasn't involved with the event. Posters for the Showcase touted it as a community talent show at a local high school theater. The Hummingbird Gardens dance class would be one act among several.

"I even brought energy cookies," the cookie lady said. *What's her name again?* The small, gray-haired woman barely peeked above the edge of the service counter. She lifted a plate of delectable-looking iced oatmeal cookies for Brie to admire.

"Are you sure about the time?" Brie asked. "Or maybe Lovey is just running late?"

"Definitely not," Sam Slate insisted. The gender-neutral senior could perform as either the male or female partner in the dance class, as needed "Arriving late is not her style. Lovey is missing."

Brie swallowed hard, trying to control her growing alarm.

"Let's not jump to conclusions," she told the group. "I'm sure she's okay."

Diana slammed her palms onto Brie's service counter. "We're worried! You need to do something!"

A few seniors balled their fists and shook them toward Brie.

*Isn't this supposed to be a season of love?* Not that Brie had any personal experience in that department. Strong emotions stirred up plenty of drama.

This close to Valentine's Day, lovesick crazies were everywhere. Jilted lovers turned murderers. Brie's mind played back the true crime podcast she had been listening to a few moments ago. The Romeo and Juliet Killers had been captured recently. *From sweethearts to eating hearts.* Brie shivered at their cannibal tales.

She had to come up with a solution for the seniors peering at her across the service desk before things turned ugly.

*Calm down, Brie. Don't let them draw you into their wild assumptions.*

"Maybe Lovey forgot about your 'emergency' session," Brie suggested. *Having a senior moment.* "I have her number. Just a second."

Brie dialed Lovey using the front desk phone. Lovey's voicemail message said, *"The subscriber's voicemail is full."* Brie hung up.

Lovey was a local celebrity. *The Elvira of romance movies.* Instead of screening horror movies like the femme fatale Elvira, who attended high school in Colorado Springs, Lovey hosted sticky-sweet romance movies, usually musicals, with guaranteed happy endings. It made sense that she screened her calls. Maybe her fans got hold of her number and filled up her inbox. Brie pulled out her smartphone and sent Lovey a text.

"Hopefully she responds to my message." Brie returned her phone to the kangaroo pocket on the front of her HMCA hoodie.

"It's not like her to ever miss a class," Layton said. "And so close to the Showcase, too!"

"I don't think she lives inside the main building like most of us," Diana said.

The stately Hummingbird Gardens was a mature structure that had been built in the late 1800s, and converted into modern apartments. But there were six individual cottages on the expansive, heavily-treed property for those who wanted more space and seclusion than apartments could provide.

"Lovey's cottage is near mine," Layton said. "It was an

awful walk here this afternoon. And the snow is coming down much heavier now."

"What if she slipped and fell out there?" George Saito exclaimed in his gravelly voice. The fuzzy ring of white hair circling his bald head looked electrified, sticking out in a dozen directions. His thick mustache quivered. "I've seen the dark underbelly of Colorado Springs with my own eyes. Bad things happen to seniors every day. We have to search for her!"

The entire dance class followed the retired detective toward the exit in a chorus of clacking canes and squeaky rollator wheels. Brie ran from behind her desk and threw herself in front of the entrance doors, her arms spread wide.

"Hold on," Brie said in alarm. The last thing she needed was for a group of unstable seniors to go out into a blizzard. "I'll go look for her myself. You guys stay here."

"Brie can't be any better at finding missing persons than her father," George said. "Locating Lovey is a job for the police."

"Isn't it a little soon to involve the fuzz?" Diana asked. She looked tense, then glanced at George. "No offense, Detective Saito."

He peered up at Diana from his hunched posture over his rollator handles, deepening his frown.

"Meow!" Professor Fluffingston, a fluffy orange Persian cat in a harness, sauntered up and rubbed his head against the gathering of legs and walking aids. Poppy Prince, the assistant manager of Hummingbird Gardens, followed behind her cat, holding his leash. Her long red frizzy hair complemented the Professor's coat. A new set of metal braces in the forty-something's mouth gleamed under the fluorescent lights.

Brie still suspected Poppy had something to do with Barry Strong's disappearance last month. And now Lovey's dance class believed another senior was missing.

"Poppy, we need you to check on a resident," George's raspy voice commanded.

Brie frowned. *He thinks* she's *more reliable than* me?

*Poppy might have kidnapped Lovey.*

"We're afraid she might have fallen down on an icy sidewalk," the cookie lady said.

"I'd go." Poppy pushed her oversized glasses up her lightly freckled nose. "But you remember the last time the Professor went out in the snow."

Brie wished she could forget searching for the cat in that storm. *Is Lovey lost in* this *storm? Where are you?*

"It took me days to get the Professor's fur refluffed after that horrible incident," Poppy sniffed.

"Then you can teach the jazz class," Brie said. *That will keep the prime suspect out of my way while I investigate.* She grabbed her coat and headed toward the door to look for Lovey.

"I can't do that," Poppy said, her voice dripping with disdain. "Professor Fluffingston is not a fan of *that* kind of dancing. Where's their instructor?"

"That's what we've been trying to tell you. Lovey's class believes she's missing," Brie said.

"Yeah! Where's Lovey?" The seniors cranked up their volume.

"Lovey?" Poppy said. "Why didn't you say that in the first place? She's at some event in Denver every day this week. Something called the 'Ripped Bodice Romance' convention."

"Is she actually staying in Denver?" George asked. "If she's commuting, we can work with her when she gets back home."

The biggest events in the region were often held in the Mile-High City. Denver was only an hour's drive from Colorado Springs, and thousands of people commuted daily between the two towns for work.

"You think she'll drive home from Denver in this weather?" Poppy asked.

"Maybe," Brie said hopefully.

"Lovey doesn't have a car," Sam said.

"Then it's settled." Poppy put her hands on her hips. "She must have used a ride share or the commuter bus to get to

Denver, and gotten a hotel room."

The senior collective grumbled.

"Why didn't she just tell us?" Diana asked, waving her hands. "Why isn't she answering her phone?"

"If Lovey's on a panel right now," Layton said, "maybe she silenced it."

"She's not obligated to tell us her plans." Poppy shrugged. "Hummingbird Gardens is an independent living facility. Lovey can come and go as she pleases."

"That's awfully rude of her," George grumbled.

"I still need my exercise," Layton complained. "I don't want to just sit here and wait for Lovey to return."

"Maybe a substitute can teach our class?" Diana suggested.

The group turned to stare at Brie expectantly.

"Wait, me? Teach the class?" Brie asked.

"Why not?" Diana asked. "You work here."

They all nodded.

*Do these old folks think I can dance just because I'm half-black? Diana and Layton shouldn't have that kind of bias. Maybe it's because I'm in my mid-twenties.*

"I'm not good at dancing—" Brie started.

"It's okay," Sam said. "You don't have to be. We have a video of our routine. We just need someone to direct us through it."

It didn't sound too bad. Brie could probably handle it.

"I'm still upset with Lovey for abandoning us in our time of need," Layton said, "but at least we know she's safe."

"This situation still doesn't sit right with me," the cookie lady said softly. "I would prefer to hear from Lovey herself."

Brie felt the same way. This whole scenario reminded her of Barry's "vacation" last month. They were trusting Poppy's information, and Brie didn't trust Poppy at all.

"Fine. I'll teach the class," Brie said, trying not to sound huffy. "But I agree that we need to hear from Lovey ourselves to make sure she's okay. I know someone I can call to contact her."

"Don't tell me," George said, a sour expression twisting his white mustache to one side. "The most inept PI in Colorado Springs. Your father."

# 3

# ❋ Thorne ❋

Thorne Bramble slouched on the seat of Chandos, his 2012 base model Ford Fusion named after the famous PI and author. As a private investigator, Thorne needed the anonymity of the white, older sedan. In truth, he couldn't afford anything newer or flashier if he'd wanted it.

He lovingly patted the dashboard. *I should probably think about getting you that oil change I've been promising.* How many months past due was it? The reminder sticker had fallen off the windshield a long time ago. Today's gig might give him the funds to finally do some maintenance.

*Mortgage first. Maintenance later.*

His tight budget wouldn't allow for splurging on fancy coffee drinks while he was on surveillance. He lifted his insulated mug of hot coffee he brought from home. The steaming liquid slid right past his lips, splashing his tongue like a lava flow.

"Hot! Hot!" The pain on Thorne's tongue was quickly replaced by a throbbing, retexturizing sensation. *Great. It's burned. I won't be able to taste anything for the rest of the day.* It was like his tongue had been replaced by a roll of flannel.

Movement distracted Thorne from his travails. The garage door of the house he was observing raised up. His car's window was flecked with snow and steamed up from his warm breath and molten coffee. He rolled the window down, hoping Gibley, the subject of his surveillance, didn't hear it.

Thorne's barely functioning phone blared with an incoming call. *Ugh!* He thought he'd silenced it while he was spying on the man. He brushed his fingers across the brittle, cracked screen, and muted his phone now. Whoever had been so rude as to interrupt Thorne's investigation could wait.

Through a curtain of falling snow, he watched a man step outside with a shovel.

Bend. Scoop. Lift. Throw to the side.

*Well, well, well, Mr. Gibley. Seems the broken sparrow can still fly.*

Gibley was performing seriously strenuous labor for a man who claimed he was incapacitated. The insurance company would be grateful to see the scammer in action.

And Thorne would be grateful to earn a paycheck. The PI business hadn't been as financially rewarding as his former corporate job as Head of Regional Legacy Product Sales for Warehouse Amalgamated Appliance Apparatuses.

*But this new gig is definitely more exciting than being a desk jockey at WAAA.*

Thorne snapped photos with his phone, then switched to video, proving the afflicted Mr. Gibley never paused to rub his supposedly aching back between shovel loads. No, he tore after the deep snow with the speed and efficiency of a snowblower.

*I should hire this guy to shovel out* my *driveway.*

Thorne's back still ached from digging out this morning. And by the time he got home this evening, all his hard work would be undone by the brief afternoon blizzard. But he wouldn't have been able to shovel all that snow without Barry's weight training. Thorne was glad his good buddy Barry Strong had returned to the HMCA gym. The guy decided to move in with some family members no one had heard him talk about before.

*Good for Barry.* Thorne was just glad the guy was okay and was still instructing Thorne in how to tame his dad bod.

Gibley shoveled his entire driveway and the sidewalk in front of his house. Then he drove away in his BMW.

Thorne rolled up his window. He checked his phone to see if his earlier caller had left a message.

*Brie!*

His daughter rarely called. Thorne could kick himself for not answering. He played the message.

"Dad, Lovey Dearheart didn't show up to teach her class this afternoon. Everyone's worried about her. Poppy claims she's at a romance convention in Denver, but Lovey isn't responding to texts or calls. Can you do a welfare check, or whatever it's called? We need to know she's okay."

Thorne shuddered. Lovey was a sexy old lady who always embarrassed him with her flirting. The woman was nearly two decades older than his fifty years. He dreaded showing up on her doorstep and getting hit on.

*Don't worry. She's probably not home, anyway.* A romance convention seemed a likely place for Lovey to be. He wasn't sure what such an event entailed, but he was pretty sure Lovey wasn't the kind of woman to miss out on an opportunity to shake her goodies for a crowd.

However, Thorne's gut roiled uncomfortably. It didn't agree with the logical conclusion, and Thorne always trusted his gut. The easy explanation may be just the surface of an iceberg, while the hard icy truth remained hidden beneath a snowy veil of mystery.

*And, Brie asked me for help.*

He was flattered that his daughter actually trusted him with an important request. He texted Brie he was available, then started Chandos and made his way toward Hummingbird Gardens. Completing his report for the insurance company could wait until Monday.

*This could be another missing senior case.*

# 4

# ✳ Lovey ✳

Lovey blinked her eyes. Though they were open, they refused to see.

*I slipped on the snowy sidewalk and hit my head. I've got a concussion. Or maybe I had a stroke?*

Fear shivered up her spine. Both of those disasters could be responsible for her sudden loss of vision. She blinked. A faint bit of light filtered through the tight weave of a fabric.

The shocking memory of a hood being dropped over her head sent Lovey into renewed panic. When she considered the bleak alternatives for her sudden blindness, her fear subsided, just a touch. *No stroke*. She couldn't see because her head was inside the black hood. But that realization dredged up a frightening chapter from her Las Vegas showgirl past.

*This is just like the time that Everett "Endgame" threw me in the trunk of his Caddie and held me prisoner.*

Endgame couldn't be responsible for her current situation. He had retired to that big casino in the sky several years ago. Even if he were still alive and pining for Lovey, there weren't enough roses, diamonds, or fancy chocolates in the world to make Lovey fall for him. But she did owe Endgame a thank you. Without him, she would have missed out on some of her happiest years. Her destiny had been tied to Endgame's henchman: the love of her life. *Bono.*

Bono had helped Lovey escape. Shortly afterward, they eloped. Bono had died too soon when a group of overly enthusiastic fans trampled him to death, thinking he was the famous musician from U2.

Lovey's next two husbands didn't work out, either. She wrinkled her nose at the thought of them and the monthly alimony payments she doled out. She was supposedly an expert on love. How could she have read them both so wrong?

Unlike the time she had been kidnapped by that thug, Endgame, Lovey was in a much more comfortable situation. She definitely wasn't in the trunk of a '70s model Cadillac.

Her faux fur-encased arms were bound behind her back with what felt like loosely tied soft, silky cords. Her ankles were tied as well, but over the cushioning of her fleece-lined snow boots. Lovey was lying on what felt like a pile of fluffy pillows. From the motion rocking her back and forth, she had to be in a moving vehicle.

The road felt pitted, but not nearly rough enough to be a rutted Nevada desert road. *Maybe I'm still in Colorado.* The shushing and thunking of windshield wipers meant it must still be snowing.

*I've definitely been kidnapped. Again.*

Unless Endgame was back from the dead, someone new had nabbed Lovey. Had one of her aggressive fans tipped over the edge from admiration to possession?

*Perhaps that obnoxious Demetrius Foxglove? Superfan and nutcase.*

"Let me go!" Lovey yelled. "This is totally unacceptable, young man!"

"I'm not a man." The voice was mechanical. Muted. But definitely female.

Lovey remembered thinking the person who grabbed her was a woman.

"Kidnapping is a serious offense," Lovey said. "If you let

me go now, I won't call the police."

"Relax," the voice said.

That was absolutely the wrong thing to say to a woman in distress. Lovey let out a wild scream.

"Hush now." The female with the distorted voice spoke from the front of the vehicle.

Lovey bit back another scream. The woman's words were oddly persuasive. Lovey writhed on her pile of pillows. She pounded the back of the car seat in front of her with her knees, not ready to accept being snatched off the sidewalk without a fight.

"Let me go!"

"Be careful back there. You might hurt yourself."

*Or Duchess.* Lovey stopped struggling, concerned she might be crushing her puppy.

"Duchess?" No response. No whining or squirming. "Where is my dear little dog?"

"I saw no animals with you."

Lovey's heart pounded hard. *Did she really blow away?*

"My miniature poodle," Lovey said past trembling lips. "She goes everywhere with me."

"You didn't leave her home during the blizzard?" the woman asked.

"Of course not!" Lovey's heart throbbed with panic. "You really didn't see her? She's pink!"

"I will look for her," the woman said.

"We need to look right now!" Lovey cried.

"As soon as I have delivered you to safety, I assure you, I will find the dog. It is a ninja's promise."

*A ninja's promise?* Must be some new slang she hadn't heard yet.

Lovey tried to calm herself. *Duchess must have hidden when she sensed danger. Poodles are already smart dogs, and Duchess is the cream of the crop. She knows where she lives.* If the pup was in trouble, she could run back home and slip through the doggy door. And if she didn't go home, Duchess would try to get help for Lovey. Any Hummingbird Gardens resident who scooped Duchess up would figure out Lovey was missing and call the police. *She can't truly be lost.* Lovey wouldn't let herself believe the worst. *Duchess is going to be all right.*

"Duchess is alone, out in the cold. She'll freeze to death!" Lovey poured on the drama. If her assailant felt guilty enough, maybe she would take Lovey home and repent for her crimes. It happened in movies all the time.

"I will deliver the dog to you. There is nothing to fear."

Lovey huffed out an exasperated breath. "Nothing to fear? I'll be the judge of that!"

Lovey struggled to identify the distorted voice. Perhaps this was one of her former fellow dancers from back in her days as a Las Vegas showgirl. *Although, they'd all be in their sixties and seventies now.* Surely, they were done with old grudges. The only remaining possibility was that her stalker must have a female working for him.

The woman continued, "I have no intention of harming you, and I would be devastated if you hurt yourself. Be not afraid, for you are in the safest of hands. A ninja can sew using spider silk for thread."

Lovey stilled. *She said it again. A ninja? I've been kidnapped by a ninja?* If Foxglove didn't hire her, could this woman be a deranged fan playing a bizarre role?

"What is it that you want? An autograph, a list of my favorite things, a lock of my hair, perhaps?" Lovey had dealt with creepy fans before. They fell in love with the personality she created for cable TV. The lovesick, flirty woman she had once played, wearing lacy gowns with a little too much cleavage showing, announced romance movies. "I'm sure we can be friends someday, but this whole kidnapping thing isn't making me fond of you."

"Ninjas have no friends," the woman said flatly. "I only seek to complete my assignment."

Lovey shuddered. "And what would that be?"

"To make sure your Valentine's Days are happy for the rest of your life."

"I'm having trouble believing you," Lovey said.

There was no evil undercurrent in the "ninja's" words. It was as though the woman honestly believed that kidnapping Lovey would make her happy. That had been true for Everett "Endgame," too. She'd had help escaping *his* clutches. This time, she could only rely on herself.

"I'm already happy. I have a wonderful life. I want to go home to my cottage. Right now!"

"You will understand everything soon enough. But at this moment, we must discuss the terms of the contract."

"Contract?" Was this so-called ninja a contracted assassin? *I've read this situation entirely wrong. I'm in extreme danger!* Lovey's breath became labored.

"You are being placed where true happiness will bloom in your life. People are like plants in new soil: it takes time to form roots. Your one-week trial period begins now. If you or my clients are dissatisfied with the arrangement, you are free to go and return to your lonely life."

Lovey still didn't understand. "But, I'm not lonely!" Lovey tried to sound sure of herself. "I have Duchess. She's all that I need. Take me home to her."

Only stony silence followed.

The ninja's talk about planting and roots made Lovey think of permanent interment in the earth. Yet there was mention of happiness blooming. None of it made sense. *Should I be terrified, or excited?*

The windshield wipers continued their slapping, the tires shushing through slush.

*Where is this woman taking me?*

Endgame had insisted he could make all of Lovey's dreams come true. She had barely escaped from that horrifying experience back in the '70s. *Now I'm almost seventy . . .*

*I will escape this new "happiness" this ninja person is threatening me with. Hopefully, with both my life and my dignity intact.*

# 5

# ✳ Thorne ✳

*An unpaid job.* Well, it wasn't like Thorne didn't have time to spare. And maybe helping out his daughter would score him some dad points. He hadn't completed his New Year's resolution of healing his relationship with his daughter yet, and Valentine's Day was a week away.

Lovey missing dance class might be a clue to something more serious going on. Abandoning her students was not Lovey's style.

*Just because she didn't show up doesn't mean she's dead in a ditch.*

After collecting the available facts from Brie at her HMCA desk late Sunday afternoon, Thorne's concern lessened. There was an existing and very logical explanation for Lovey's disappearance. The lure of the Ripped Bodice Romance convention would be hard for a former star like Lovey to resist.

After all, Barry Strong had vanished without telling anyone he was leaving, and he was just fine. He had even repaid Thorne for his worries with *two* celery juices. Though Barry still wouldn't share the details of his reunion with this mystery family, he was happier than Thorne had ever seen the old guy.

Thorne headed straight for the office Ramona Grant shared with Poppy Prince. Brie didn't trust Poppy, but all Thorne had learned about the redhead during a past investigation was that she really liked cats. *And who doesn't like cats?*

The person he really needed to speak to was Ramona Grant, the senior property manager of Hummingbird Gardens. Senior as in the top boss, not as in elderly. *We're almost the same age.* Thorne had taken note of her birthday the last time they spoke. He didn't expect Ramona to share any useful information with him. After his experience searching for Barry, he knew Ramona carefully guarded the privacy of Hummingbird Gardens residents. He would need to use his PI skills to learn where Lovey resided.

*If I have to, I'll pilfer a key.*

Thorne adjusted the collar of his winter trenchcoat and pulled his brown leather gloves on a little tighter. He cocked his tan fedora to one side. *I need to look official. And it wouldn't hurt to look my best for Ramona.* Just thinking about the beautiful woman increased his heart rate. He put on a winning smile and walked through the entryway.

"Hello," a woman with a frizzy mane of long red hair greeted him. He had seen her in pictures with her cat online during his previous missing senior case. The majestic beast regularly sauntered around Hummingbird and the HMCA, but Thorne had never focused on the feline's human traveling companion in real life. It was the cat that held his attention. The large, fluffy Persian was an eye-catching shade of orange.

"Hi, you're Poppy, correct?" Thorne waved. "And Doctor Fluffy?"

"His name is Professor Fluffingston," Poppy corrected him.

The Professor lifted his head from napping and said, "meow," matter-of-factly. He closed his golden eyes and put his smushed nose down on his paws again.

*Such a classy guy. A man could learn a thing or two from a cat like that.*

"Is there something you need from me?" Poppy asked. She licked her lips slowly and batted her eyelashes.

"Actually, I was looking for Ramona," Thorne said.

"I saw her a little while ago. She's around here somewhere, but maybe *I* can help you?" Poppy licked her lips again.

Thorne understood why she kept doing that. He knew the feeling well. The dry climate of the Rocky Mountain foothills sucked all the moisture right out of a person.

"Here." Thorne handed her an unopened lip balm with the HMCA logo on it. He often took one from the basket of free stuff on Brie's desk. That was also where all of his ink pens came from, and his key chain. "I always keep a few of these with me. Colorado Springs in winter is so dry, even with the snow. You can never have enough lip balm."

"Um, thanks," Poppy said with a frown. "So thoughtful." She opened it and applied it slowly to her pink lips, batting her eyes again as she did so.

*Maybe her eyes are dry, too. Whelp, I can't help with that!* Brie's desktop goody basket didn't offer free eye drops.

"Anyway, have you seen Lovey Dearheart? I've been hired to contact her." Thorne was basically telling the truth. He flashed his private investigator business card at Poppy for a second and quickly returned it to his wallet. People sometimes assumed he had more legal authority than he really did when he showed them his card. "Have you spoken to her recently?"

"She's not missing."

"I didn't say she was missing," Thorne said. Maybe Brie was right about this woman being sketchy.

"Lovey is at a romance convention. Brie asked about her, too." Poppy explained, "She's the girl that works the HMCA front desk."

"Brie is my daughter," Thorne said stiffly. He was used to people failing to see the resemblance, even though she looked more like him than her mother.

"Oh? But—" Poppy started.

"But what?" Thorne raised an eyebrow. Surely she wasn't going to comment on their differences in skin coloring and hair texture.

"You're much too young to be Brie's father!" Poppy smiled, revealing an impressive rack of braces. The woman had to be in her forties, but Thorne had known other adults who got their teeth straightened later in life. "Were you a teen dad?"

"Ha ha, no." Thorne's past relationship with alcohol hadn't done him any favors. He looked every day of his fifty years. But he still considered himself dashing for a middle-aged guy. Plus, his workouts with Barry must be paying off. He had almost forgotten what it was like to be flirted with. *Still got it. Too bad Ramona isn't here.*

Thorne got back to the important subject at hand. "If Lovey is at this convention, why isn't she answering her phone? I'd like to verify that she actually left Colorado Springs. Lovey lives alone. What if she fell at home, is injured, and can't reach her phone? What's her room number?"

Poppy looked genuinely alarmed. "Lovey doesn't live in the main building. She's in Cottage 1. Hold on a second." She opened a lockbox and pulled out a key. "Now you've got me really worried. Do you mind coming with me to check on her?"

*Nice!* This was going so much easier than Thorne anticipated. Poppy was extremely cooperative. Maybe she wasn't guilty of wrongdoing.

"Well, this isn't normal protocol." Thorne tried to sound official. If Lovey wasn't home, he wanted to poke around in her belongings for clues about where she went. He didn't need Poppy there, cramping his style. "I usually work alone. Like, you know. A lone wolf." He cocked his head to one side as he stared off into an imaginary distance full of wild creatures. His fedora slid. He clapped a hand to his hat, smashing it in place on his gray-streaked brown hair. "If Lovey is in some kind of distress, or is, uh, you know, deceased, then—"

"Oh! Right! You can go by yourself, Mr. Lone Wolf." Poppy winked. "Seeing a dead human body would distress the Professor. And, I don't like leaving the Professor on his own.

There are too many girl cats wandering around unsupervised, trying to lead him astray. Do you mind going alone?"

"No problemo," Thorne said, taking the key.

Thorne had learned from his online research that the studly cat wasn't "fixed." *The Professor is a real man's cat,* Thorne thought with admiration.

"I'll bring back a full report," Thorne assured Poppy as he exited the office.

The afternoon blizzard had dumped its load of snow and moved on. Thorne walked across the crunchy sidewalk pockmarked with de-icing salt. The Hummingbird Gardens Senior Apartments towered behind him. Local Colorado red sandstone and white limestone contrasted dramatically, emphasizing the Victorian era architecture. Balconies on the second and third floors completed the elegant look. A small distance from the remodeled vintage apartment building, individual cottages shared the tree-lined, park-like property

Before Thorne reached the door to Cottage 1, he heard yipping noises.

"Lovey?" Thorne called out. Maybe the weird sound was coming from the old woman writhing in pain. Hopefully, she hadn't fallen in the shower. Thorne had already seen more of Lovey's body than he ever needed to. He shuddered and took a deep breath. "I'm coming in!"

He turned the key and stepped inside. A pink toy poodle dressed in a fur coat and boots raced out like a hound from heck, barking so forcefully it involuntarily jumped with every sound. *Good. It wasn't Lovey making that noise.* Thorne took off his leather glove and put his hand down for the dog to sniff. It immediately coated Thorne's hand in saliva.

"Hey, dog. Good dog. Where's your mistress?" Thorne asked, hoping the pup would lead him Lassie-style to Lovey. But the dog just kept licking. *And this is why I'm a cat person.*

Thorne stood and made a sweep of the place, checking every room for Lovey. She wasn't there. The dog's kibble dish was empty, and its water was only half full. But its pee pad didn't have any deposits drying on the surface. Lovey couldn't have been gone more than a few hours.

Thorne took a deeper dive into Lovey's disappearance. A pile of letters sat on an end table. Thorne examined one. It was unopened, but Thorne thought he recognized the name on the return address: Demetrius Foxglove. *Where have I seen this name before?*

Thorne picked a few more letters from beneath the top one. They all had the same return address as the first. Thorne was itching to know what was in the envelopes, but none of them had been opened. He held one of the letters up to a light, but it was inside a security envelope. Committing mail fraud seemed like a bad idea. Thorne took a photo of the mail with his phone and restacked the letters.

Was this Foxglove person stalking Lovey? Did he have something to do with her disappearance? Maybe the guy forced her to go to the convention, and now wouldn't let her answer her phone.

The dog brought its leash to Thorne. Maybe it didn't want to use the pee pad. Thorne took the hint and attached the leash to its collar. A red flower decoration fell off. He stuck it back on. The poodle was already dressed for cold weather, which seemed odd. Why would Lovey leave her dog indoors wearing a winter coat and booties? The cottage was plenty warm for an animal covered in curly fur. He let the pup lead him out the front door and locked it behind him.

Instead of finding a spot in the snow to piddle, the dog went snuffling along. It took Thorne to a set of footprints that went off the sidewalk and into the snow. The temperatures had been too cold to melt the tracks. The poodle *was* just like Lassie.

"Take me to Lovey," Thorne commanded. And they were off. From what he could deduce from the spacing between the footprints, Lovey had been walking. She hadn't been running from danger.

Thorne's open winter trenchcoat did nothing to prevent cold from seeping freely beneath it. Despite Barry's help, Thorne still couldn't button his overcoat. So the garment was more for style than practical use. Half the job of being a PI was looking the part. Thorne wrapped the flaps of the coat tighter around himself. He gritted his chattering teeth and pressed on.

Suddenly, the footprints stopped in the middle of a pristine white snowfield. Like whoever was walking there had been abducted by aliens.

*Or Brie's imaginary ninja?*

Thorne stepped carefully through the surrounding snow-covered lawn. There were no other indentations, besides the dainty boot prints Lovey had left.

This situation needed a more thorough investigation. Poppy expected him to return the key to Lovey's cottage before her office closed. Thorne decided to get a copy of the key to Cottage 1 made at the hardware store. He needed continued access in case something bad had happened to Lovey, and his missing person search turned into a murder investigation.

"What do I do with you?" he asked the poodle.

The tiny creature shivered despite its winter coat. It stared up at Thorne with trust in its shiny dark eyes.

"Okay, you can go with me."

Last month, Thorne had struggled with deodorizing his vehicle after a broccoli incident. He hoped the dog wouldn't stink up Chandos again. *Dogs are smelly, right?* Happily, they reached the store without additional insult to Chandos's aroma.

Walking through the aisles of the hardware store with the fuzzy pink poodle attracted a lot of attention.

"How sweet!" A hot chick bent down and let the dog paint her hand in slobber. "What's her name?"

*Huh. The dog is a her.* Thorne really knew nothing about dogs. "Um, Pinkie," Thorne said. That sounded like a reasonably girly name.

"Awww!" Three more smoking hot ladies came to admire

the dog.

Why were there so many good-looking gals at the hardware store? *I'm a real chick magnet today.* Between Poppy and these women, Thorne was beginning to think he was irresistible. But being realistic, the poodle was what drew female attention at an increased rate. He wasn't a dog person, but now he could see the appeal.

Thorne briefly considered asking for one dog-admiring woman's phone number, but he wasn't really interested in dating someone not much older than his daughter.

On the way to the checkout counter, Thorne saw something he couldn't pass up on an endcap: pepper spray. *Brie needs a new one of these.* Thorne could still taste pepper from the canister she emptied last month. He might as well invest in a fresh one for himself, too. He picked out a bright pink one for Brie, and a no-frills, manly black one for himself.

After making his purchases, Thorne returned to Hummingbird Gardens and took the dog back to Lovey's cottage. His new key worked. Stepping inside, he called out for Lovey. The old lady still wasn't home.

Then he noticed that the dog's food dish and water had been refilled. Had Lovey returned to her cottage while Thorne was away?

He slipped into PI stealth mode and crept around the cottage again, looking for more clues. New letters, postmarked for today, were perched on top of the stack of stalker mail. *Someone dropped off the mail while I was gone.*

A new thought occurred to Thorne. Assuming Lovey was at the convention, she must have asked her friend Sam to check in on the dog.

He shook his head. *I've been worried about nothing.* Hopefully, Sam wasn't worried or out looking for the pup.

Thorne backed out, being careful to keep the dog out of harm's way, although she seemed frantic to go with him.

"Sorry, girl. But Sam will be back soon."

He examined the doggy door. Until he knew more, he couldn't risk the poodle running away. There was a latch. He fastened it.

When Thorne closed the door, the poodle yipped and cried, her painted toenails scraping against the inside of the door.

Thorne steeled himself against her cuteness and trudged to Ramona and Poppy's office to return Lovey's key.

Poppy stood to greet him. "Oh, good, you're back!"

Professor Fluffingston hopped down from a fancy cat bed on top of Poppy's desk and rubbed his orange body against Thorne's legs. Thorne reached down to pet the classy animal, but Poppy stopped him.

"Ah ah ah," she said. "Safety first." She held up a bottle of hand sanitizer.

"Right! Sorry!" Thorne took his gloves off and neutralized his toxic hands. His fingertips burned from where his cracked phone screen must have cut him. The pain subsided when he put his hands on the softest fur on the planet.

*Yep. I'm still a cat guy.*

"Good news, Lovey's not dead in her cottage," Thorne said.

"Thank goodness! I'm so glad you checked." Poppy took the original key from Thorne.

"What's this about?" Ramona asked.

"Oh, hi Ramona." Thorne felt his face flush. He had been so distracted by the Professor, he hadn't noticed her enter the office. She was gorgeous as ever, but all business. Thorne swallowed, and with Herculean effort, he found the words to respond to Ramona. "I've been looking for Lovey Dearheart."

"Her pet sitter said she'll be back from the convention next week," Ramona said.

"Pet sitter?" Thorne asked. "Her friend Sam isn't watching the dog?"

"I don't think so," Ramona said.

"Oh, Thorne. See? Everything's fine," Poppy huffed. "I can't believe you got me all worked up for nothing."

*Yikes! I had the dog with me at the hardware store when the sitter came by.* He scratched his stubble-coated chin. Then why didn't the sitter run to the office in a panic? Thorne's gut rumbled. This whole pet sitter thing didn't sit right. *I always trust my gut.* Neither woman had mentioned this sitter reporting a missing poodle. And there was still the question of Lovey not responding to friends' frantic calls.

"Why isn't Lovey answering her phone?" Thorne asked.

"If I was surrounded by adoring fans, I wouldn't answer my phone, either." Poppy looked up into the air with a dreamy expression "I often ignore calls and texts when the Professor is at a cat fancier event."

"Lovey might have forgotten her charger," Ramona said. "Happens all the time around here."

The two women had not given him satisfactory answers. Instead, Thorne only had more questions. And even more disappointing, Ramona seemed to be the only woman in Colorado Springs immune to his charms today.

"I've gotta go." Thorne tipped his fedora and left. He performed his finest PI slinking moves back to Lovey's cottage. What if the pet sitter and Lovey's stalker were one and the same person?

Outside Lovey's door, he could hear the pink pooch whining. She poked her head out of the doggy door. *She unlatched the doggy door? Or did the stalker do it?*

*What if the dog-sitter is inside right now?*

Thorne briefly considered calling the police. But by the time they got there, it might be too late.

*Looks like this lone wolf has some prey to catch.*

Thorne held up one hand, palm facing the doggy door. "Heel!" he whispered. *That's a dog thing, right?* It must have been. The whining quieted.

Thorne pulled the brand-new canister of pepper spray from his pocket. He quietly tried the doorknob. Locked. He used his key and leapt through the doorway, pepper spray aimed to attack whoever lurked in the late afternoon shadows.

He cleared each room. No one was there but the pup. But Thorne's gut was still talking to him. He went directly to the mail and sifted through the new letters. In between an envelope full of local coupons and a credit card offer, there was a flyer for Demetrius Foxglove's Love Parlor and Sir Lancelot's Videography Services. *Foxglove.*

The Love Parlor's logo was deceptively cutesy. A girl fox and boy fox faced away from each other, their tails forming a heart between them.

Had Foxglove kidnapped Lovey, then come back for her little dog, while Thorne was at the hardware store? If only the dog could tell him what had happened to her mistress.

The pup stared up at Thorne with her big brown eyes. Her black button nose wriggled on her sweet pink face. All alone until Lovey or the so-called dog-sitter returned. *If anyone returns.*

*Darn it.*

The pink poodle was vital to this case.

"Come on, little dog." Thorne patted his thigh. "You're coming home with me."

It was only after he got home Sunday night that Thorne realized he should have grabbed some dog food, instead of just taking the animal's clothes and bed. He set down a cereal bowl full of water on the kitchen floor for the poodle. But there wasn't a crumb of animal food in his house.

*Maybe I should go back.* But appearing at the cottage again could put him and the pup in danger if the stalker returned. Plus, it would attract the wrong kind of attention. It wasn't as if he was legally authorized to be in Lovey's cottage. Besides, he had plenty of hamburger in the freezer, and boxes of an Angus Assistant noodle and sauce mix to cook with it. *A perfectly balanced meal for man and dog.*

At bedtime, the little poodle whined until he lifted her onto his bed. It was pleasant having a warm body to share the queen mattress with him. Until the dog grunted. A cloud of funk enveloped Thorne.

# 6

# ✳ Brie ✳

Brie had been worried ever since her father called her last night. He found Duchess without Lovey, which was very troubling. The two were inseparable. The only thing keeping Brie from calling Officer Riggs was protecting her father from prosecution. *Breaking and entering. Not to mention dog-napping.*

Plus, her father had a tendency to exaggerate. Thinking rationally, the facts lined up with the most logical explanation: Lovey had to be at the Ripped Bodice Romance convention. She must have hired a pet sitter, like Ramona told Brie's father, because maybe dogs weren't allowed there.

Unable to sleep, she had spent a couple of hours before bed working through online dance tutorials. She taught herself how to do jazz squares, chassés, and reviewed the Electric Slide for what felt like a hundred times. She remembered trying to learn the line dance in an elementary school gym class with disastrous results. *Poor Simon.* His foot was never the same after that.

She was desperate to replace the Electric Slide song virus she had contracted. It wasn't the whole song afflicting her. Just the words, "It's electric! Boogie woogie, woogie!" playing over and over in her mind.

Brie entered the classroom where Lovey's Monday morning

class had gathered bright and early. Old ladies and gentlemen crowded around Brie.

"Is Lovey back?" Sam asked. Despite their impressive collection of flashy costumes, the senior always dressed blandly. Today, Sam wore gray sweats and a tan shirt over their shapeless body. "I still haven't heard from her."

The rest of the seniors murmured. Brie knew that Sam and Lovey were good friends. If Lovey called anyone with an update, it should be Sam.

"Not yet." Brie frowned.

"We need to practice," the cookie lady said.

"You've got that right," Layton said. The retired chef patted his tummy as he smiled at the cookie lady. "I need to burn off the calories from your most excellent peanut brittle and Valentine's cookies."

The ever-present tray of homemade goodies sat on a table. The gray-haired lady smiled.

"I need to perfect my special love cookies before the holiday. If you eat one, you're guaranteed to have love on your Valentine's Day."

She held the tray out to Brie.

"No thanks," Brie said. Her sweatpants were getting tight.

"It's okay, dear. They're gluten-free."

Did that mean they were healthy then? Brie grabbed one.

The sugar cookies were heart-shaped with red and pink sprinkles. Slightly crisp, the buttery cookie melted on Brie's tongue. It didn't taste like anything from the grocery store. Undertones of sweet almond married the strong vanilla flavor.

George interrupted Brie before she could indulge in any more of the tasty treats.

"Well?" George asked. "Do I need to notify my grandson to conduct a real search for Lovey?"

Brie almost melted at the mention of Officer Riggs Saito. He was as buttery sweet as the cookie lady's treats. Brie felt herself zoning out, as she did whenever Riggs was on her mind.

"Brie?" George snapped, causing his bushy mustache to quiver. He waved a hand in front of her face. "The girl must be stoned again. As usual. Colorado has fallen into the sewer since they decided to legalize pot here."

"I don't use marijuana, Mr. Saito," Brie said, pulling herself out of her fog. "My father is on the case." *And needs my help if he's going to make any progress.* "Hold tight, everyone. I'll call Ramona and ask if she's heard from Lovey yet. This all must be some kind of mistake."

It was out of character for Lovey to abandon her students. Not even for a romance convention. She cared too much about teaching her classes. But sometimes seniors made unexpected decisions, embracing life knowing they had fewer years ahead of them than they had behind them. Perhaps Lovey had jumped on an opportunity she felt she'd never have again.

Brie stepped out of the classroom to make the call. Ramona was an attractive forty-nine-year-old. She had a flawless light-brown complexion, like Brie. She was pretty, for an older woman. *For a woman of any age,* Brie conceded. *Too bad Dad can't hook up with someone like Ramona. Maybe he'd finally get over his divorce from Mom.*

Ramona answered after three rings. "Hummingbird Gardens Senior Apartments. Ramona speaking."

"Hi, this is Brie from the HMCA."

"Yes, Brie. How may I help you?" Ramona sounded cheerful.

"Lovey Dearheart didn't show up to teach her dance class. Do you know where she is?"

"She's attending the Ripped Bodice Romance convention," Ramona said.

"That's what Poppy told us yesterday. Have you heard from Lovey since she left?"

"No," Ramona replied. "But I don't know why she would need to call me. She has a pet sitter."

*A lousy pet sitter if they haven't reported Duchess missing.*

Brie considered mentioning that her father had Duchess. But that might get him into trouble. Brie tried a different track.

"Lovey is very private. It just doesn't seem like she'd attend a big convention."

Lovey had complained about overly enthusiastic fans. Brie shook her head. It didn't make sense for Lovey to appear at such a public event at all.

"I'm sure there's nothing to worry about." Ramona was silent for a moment. "Your father performed a welfare check yesterday, and Lovey wasn't home."

"Correct."

"So I think we can rest assured that she's at the convention. I need to get going. I have an important orientation to do. There's a new physical therapist onboarding."

"I wonder if he can teach senior dance classes," Brie said.

"He's a geriatric specialist," Ramona said, "so maybe. But not yet. We've got orientation all day."

Brie sighed. "I'll let the class know. Hopefully, Lovey shows up soon."

"Don't worry. I'm sure she's having a blast at that convention and forgot all about her class." Ramona hung up.

Brie had done what she could.

*If she's enjoying herself at that stupid convention while we're all worried about her, I'm going to be really upset.*

Brie trudged back into the HMCA classroom.

The senior class hadn't been idle during her phone call. They gyrated and thrust their hips to "You Sexy Thing," by Hot Chocolate.

*I believe in miracles . . . where you from?*

The words blared from a Bluetooth speaker at an intense volume that hurt Brie's ears. *Probably because the seniors' hearing isn't the best.*

"Ah, you're back." Layton punched the pause button on his smartphone. He swiped a handkerchief across his brow. "Where is Lovey?"

"Ramona agrees with Poppy. They both think she's at the romance convention," Brie said.

"I wonder if Lovey's family can confirm that," the cookie lady said.

"Lovey doesn't have any family besides her dog," Diana said. "Not that she's mentioned."

Sam nodded in confirmation.

*Duchess is Lovey's only family? Dad had better take that poodle back to her cottage before Lovey finds out she's missing.*

"It is peculiar," Diana continued.

"What do you mean?" Layton asked.

"Two seniors going missing from Hummingbird Gardens so far this year," Diana said.

"Should we be worried about our safety?" The cookie lady set down her tray of treats and wrung her hands together.

"Of course!" George exclaimed. "We should be terrified!"

"What can we do to protect ourselves?" Sam asked.

"Have faith, everyone. Barry's not missing anymore." Layton frowned. "Although if Lovey doesn't come back soon, we won't be ready for the Valentine's Showcase."

"Then we've got no time to waste." Diana tapped her smartwatch.

The seniors all stared at Brie.

She hoped her face didn't reflect her inner reluctance. *I really don't want to do this.*

"I suppose I can fill in again," Brie said. "Just once more."

"Terrific!" Diana handed Brie a chartreuse ostrich plume fan and matching feather boa. "Let's get busy!"

Layton punched the sound back on. The seniors watched Brie expectantly. Despite watching the video of the dance, she had no idea what they were doing. She imitated the moves on the tiny phone screen.

Hesitant at first, Brie began to groove to the pop tune that was a hit in 1976. She felt as awkward as she must have looked at age five, when she pranced across the recital stage in a tutu and tripped over her own dance slippers. At least this dance didn't require moving her feet much.

Brie did a half-squat, thrust her booty out, and bounced up and down to the rhythm of the song.

"Twerk it, girl!" Diana said.

*So that's what twerking means.*

# 7

# ✳ Lovey ✳

*This is the most comfortable bed I've ever been in.* Lovey hated to admit the truth as she pushed herself upright from a mound of frilly, pastel pink pillows. The queen mattress was just right. Not too firm, not too soft. Almost as though someone knew her exact specifications. *I just wish I'd been able to enjoy it.*

Lovey resisted falling asleep last night. *The night of my abduction.* Every time she tried the bedroom door, it was locked. From the outside.

She was a prisoner of the black-garbed ninja.

Feeble early morning winter sun illuminated the bedroom through sheer pink curtains. Lovey blinked, her eyes adjusting to the muted light in the girliest room she had ever seen. There were even more ruffles and lace than in her own bedroom in her Hummingbird Gardens cottage.

"Duchess?"

Lovey searched the spacious room again, even though she'd conducted a fruitless hunt several times last night. She even peeped inside the walk-in closet, calling softly for her puppy. The clothing bars held padded satin hangers of clothes that looked suspiciously close to her size and style. She knelt beside the bed, calling for her puppy, looking under the ruffled pink bed skirt.

The fear that had made her feel helpless last night slowly evaporated in the morning light. Anger took its place. Duchess must be terrified. *If she survived the storm. No! Don't think that way.*

Lovey was reasonably certain the intelligent doggy would have run home. *Only to find the cottage empty.* She had a puppy pee pad for emergencies, but the pink poodle was a tidy little creature. Duchess liked her routine.

This was a totally unacceptable situation.

Lovey slipped her feet into her snow boots and pulled on her fluffy pink coat. She patted the pockets for the tenth time. Her smartphone and her bag were nowhere to be found. There wasn't even an old-fashioned landline phone in the room for her to make a 911 call. *I can't rely on rescue. I must save myself.* One more thing to be angry about.

She marched to the bedroom door and grasped the handle, prepared to yell, kick, and beat with her fists to earn her freedom. When she grabbed the doorknob this time, it turned. Someone had finally unlocked it.

Lovey pulled the door open slowly, peeking out into an empty hallway. She stepped back inside, checking her appearance in the mirror above the spindle-legged vanity table. Her dance outfit was rumpled from her nearly sleepless night. She attempted to pat out the most offensive wrinkles on the pink leotard and short satin skirt. Someone had left a new comb and brush set, still in the packaging.

The closet full of clothing, the toiletries, smacked of major preplanning by some creepy stalker. She felt vulnerable.

The carpeted hallway was empty except for framed photos of a family dressed up for various romantic musical theater productions Lovey recognized: *My Fair Lady, Hello Dolly!, State Fair.* The hallway dead-ended to the left. She had no choice of direction if she was going to escape. Lovey slid along the wall, listening for danger. She stopped.

"And step two three. And step two three."

A man's voice. Now she could hear music. A show tune played. One she had danced to, once upon a time. She recognized the song from *Singin' in the Rain*. A musical. Lovey peeked around the corner. A large screen TV dominated a family room. A man, woman, and one child pranced along with dancers, twirling yellow vinyl umbrellas around. Slouched on a cushioned chair was an older child, maybe a young teen, dressed all in black with thigh-high platform boots. His arms were crossed, and a scowl creased his young face.

"Come on, Randy," the man said. "We only have time for one more practice before school."

"The name is Randall," the boy groused. The child's voice cracked, breaking between deep and high tones. No, not a child, really. But not yet a man, either. A high school-aged kid?

*He's definitely a teenager.*

In Lovey's childhood, speaking to your parents in that tone of voice resulted in dire consequences. *At least, I assume the man and woman are the boy's parents.*

"If we're going to be ready for the Valentine's Showcase," the woman said, "we need to practice our routine."

Lovey's heart nearly skipped a beat. That was the dance recital her HMCA class was going to perform in. The seniors were working so hard.

"Bruh," the seated teen, Randall, said. "*Singin' in the Rain* is dog water. I am *not* doing this."

The other three were preoccupied with the bright colors and swirling dancers on the screen.

Lovey eased her way around the corner. She could see the front door. So close, and yet it might as well have been miles away. She screwed up her courage and made a dash for it.

Her snow boots clopped loudly on the parquet flooring.

"The old lady!" Randall screamed. "She's escaping!"

The man and woman tossed their umbrellas aside, racing across the room to Lovey.

"Mom! You're awake!" Auburn hair flipped up at the

shoulders of the woman's dusty rose-colored turtleneck. She appeared to be in her mid-thirties, which would be the right age for Lovey's daughter. *If I had a daughter. Which I don't.*

"You slept right through dinner last night. You must be starved," the man said. He matched the woman with his tidy style and cheerful smile. He wore a button-down white shirt with a blue and silver striped tie under a sweater vest. They both looked like parents from some previous generation. Wholesome to a fault. "We've already had breakfast, but we saved a plate for you, Mother."

The younger child, a girl dressed in pink polka-dotted ruffles, galloped toward Lovey. She threw her little arms around Lovey's waist.

"Grandma!"

Lovey must have looked as shocked as she felt.

"This has to be quite a surprise to you," the woman said. "Come to the kitchen, and we'll explain everything."

The teenager dressed in black rolled off his chair and slouched near. He placed his hands on his hips.

"Oh, no. Another member of the pink sparkle club. Ugh! I should have gotten a say in this."

"You'd pick some nasty old witch," the girl said, clinging to Lovey. Her strawberry blond hair was pulled into two high pigtails on either side of her pink-cheeked face. "With warts and spider webs. I like this one!"

*This one?* Was Lovey a commodity? Had she been purchased by this family from the old lady store?

"Oh!" Lovey felt light-headed. She threw an arm out, pressing a hand against the wall.

"Catch her!" the woman yelled.

Lovey wasn't sure how it happened, but moments later, she was seated in a cozy, bright kitchen with her hands wrapped around a mug of Earl Grey. A huge blueberry muffin, crispy bacon, and cheesy scrambled eggs sat on a sunny yellow plate in front of her.

Two paper lunch bags sat on top of the counter. Two backpacks sat on the floor beneath them. One was pink and decorated with unicorns and rainbows. The black one was covered with frightening-looking patches displaying cartoony monsters and weird symbols.

"You don't need that coat," the woman said. "It's too warm to wear indoors. Overheating probably made you feel faint."

"No, that's not the problem at all," Lovey said. But she let the woman tug the fluffy coat off her arms. "I was overwhelmed by the reality of being held captive against my will."

"If we got a defective one," Randall said, "can we trade her in to the ninja for a better model?"

"Stop being rude," the little girl said. She held a hand out to Lovey. "Randy is acting like this because he's in puberty. He's fourteen. My name is Chrissy, I'm nine years old, and I love you, Grandma!"

Lovey wasn't sure which of the two children was more alarming. Chrissy acted much younger than her age, while Randall seemed as grumpy as an old man. Lovey accepted Crissy's warm little hand. The child grasped hold like she would never let Lovey go.

"Let your grandmother drink her tea," the woman said.

"You have the advantage of me," Lovey said. "I have no idea who you people are."

"I'm Sally Hoffman. This is my husband, Harry. And you've already met our children, Randy and Chrissy."

"I'm Randall," the boy said. "And we don't need any more sappy cheerfulness in this house."

"Then I'll try to be as bitter and dark as you, young man," Lovey snapped. "If that will earn me my freedom."

"Not for the next week," Harry said. "It's in the contract."

"Contract," Lovey said. The ninja had mentioned that before. She sipped her tea, then realized she was thirsty. And hungry. She gulped down the Earl Grey, then tore into the muffin with unladylike zeal.

"The ninja's contract," Chrissy said. "You stay with us for a week, then you become my grandma."

"I know you'll stay," Sally said. "We have so much in common. You're a perfect fit! You love romantic movies. We love romantic movies."

"Speak for yourself," Randall grumbled.

"The ninja placed you with us because of our shared interests," Harry said. "And because we have a hole in our lives that only the right grandparent can fill. You!"

"Don't you understand?" Lovey looked to the mother and father. "This is kidnapping. You're going to be in a lot of trouble. I need to go home. I have a little dog." She choked on a sob. "Duchess must be frantic by now."

"The ninja is going to get your dog," Harry said. "I'm sure she feels terrible about leaving Duchess behind. We want you to feel as comfortable as possible in your new home."

"I don't want Duchess brought here," Lovey said. "What I want is to be taken back to my cottage. To *my* home."

Sally poured another cup of tea. Lovey sipped slowly.

"You don't want to be my grandma?" Chrissy's lower lip trembled.

"This isn't one of your dumb musicals," Randall said. "There's no happily ever afters in real life."

*That's not true.* Although Lovey's own life had been slim in that category, she firmly believed in the possibility of love. Of true happiness. She'd experienced that briefly with Bono. But now was not the time to make that argument. Now was the time to escape.

"Can you tell me where the little girls' room is?" she asked Chrissy. "Elderly people have small bladders, you know." In reality, there was nothing wrong with Lovey's bladder. Dancing kept her pelvic floor muscles firm. Although she did like to wear a thin layer of protection for the occasional sneeze-leak.

Chrissy grasped her hand. "I'll show you."

Lovey glanced longingly at her furry pink coat. She hated

to leave it behind, but she couldn't alert the parents to her plan to escape by grabbing it.

After convincing Chrissy she didn't need assistance in the powder room, Lovey closed and locked the door. It was the oldest trick in the book. Lovey had escaped unwanted advances from fans more than once by ducking out a window.

This bathroom window was high on the wall. It was small, too. Given enough time, she might manage climbing up and shimmying through. There were distinct advantages to staying slim.

"Are you done yet, Grandma?" Chrissy asked.

"Just another minute," Lovey said. "Or two."

She placed a small step stool under the window. She unlatched the clasp. It was going to be strenuous, but Lovey was certain she could make it.

*Tap tap tap.* "Grandma?"

Randall spoke. "Don't you get it? The old lady's trying to escape out the window. She doesn't want to be your grandma."

"You're mean!"

Lovey hoisted her elbows onto the windowsill. It was a long way to the snow-covered ground, but she could make it without breaking any bones. *Probably.* Although the last time she'd bailed from a dicey situation by jumping out a window, Lovey had been a lot younger. At sixty-nine, a broken hip wasn't inevitable, but she couldn't deny the risk.

The chilly air sliced at her face. Her nose began dripping from the winter wind. She wished she had her coat. She didn't even know where she was, thanks to that ninja putting a hood over her head. *Cold. Lost.* Lovey rested halfway out the window, considering her options.

Then she heard Chrissy sniffling. "Grandma?"

The little girl's brother had made her cry.

*No, I made her cry.* With a frustrated sigh, Lovey lowered herself back into the bathroom.

"I'm coming."

# 8

# ✳ Thorne ✳

Monday morning, from the comfort of his home office, Thorne turned in the report for his paid gig while sipping his third, or was it his fourth, coffee of the day. *Who's counting?* He attached photographs and videos, then hit "send." Not pausing to revel in the satisfaction of nearly earning a mortgage payment, he went right back to work on his daughter's request.

He pulled out and labeled a file folder. *Missing Person Lovey Dearheart.* Paper files were definitely old school, but it felt authentically PI. *Where to start? At the beginning.*

Low-hanging fruit came first. Thorne looked up the Ripped Bodice Romance convention attendee list. It didn't seem wise to post everyone's name on the website, but most of these types of gatherings were frighteningly transparent. This convention was no different, but Lovey's name didn't come up on the list of official registrants. Lovey Dearheart was a minor celebrity in the romance world. She might register under a different name to avoid weird fans like Demetrius Foxglove, the guy flooding her mailbox.

Next, Thorne did a search for the Foxglove guy. He immediately got a hit. Thorne snapped his fingers.

"Now I remember where I've heard that name," he told the pink dog sitting at his feet.

While investigating a previous missing senior case, Thorne

had run across a website for men who had trouble finding love. Or even speaking to women. Demetrius Foxglove and his Master Class on "How to Fill Your Castle with Princesses" had been on an unsavory character's computer. Was Mr. Foxglove trying to add Lovey to his "castle"?

*Eww.* Lovey was in danger.

Thorne fed the dog his breakfast of champions: frosted corn flakes, milk, and mini powdered donuts he purchased from the gas station. He figured a dog didn't need coffee. The poodle seemed kind of hyper by nature.

After breakfast, the poodle made a face, scrunching up her doggy nose. Then it hit Thorne. He waved his hand in front of his face.

"What's your problem?" Thorne asked. Of course, the dog didn't answer. "You look so ladylike, but that is not nice at all."

Determined to solve the mystery of Lovey's disappearance and get the gas bomb dog out of his life, Thorne checked his phone's photo gallery. The cracked screen made it impossible to decipher details, so he sent a photo to his computer. He clicked on the picture he had snapped of the stack of unopened letters on Lovey's table, enlarging it. The return labels listed a street address in Old Colorado City, a few blocks west of downtown Colorado Springs.

"Time to find out what this Demetrius Foxglove character is really up to," Thorne told the dog. "We'll make him tell us where he took Lovey."

"Yip!"

Thorne drove with the windows cracked open to the cold February air. The dog shouldn't mind. It was still dressed for the weather in its little pink coat and boots. Besides, it was the dog's fault Thorne couldn't roll up the windows. How did one tiny dog create so much gas?

The return address on the envelopes wasn't fake. Thorne located the one-story red brick strip mall. Why would a stalker use their real address on an envelope if it contained anything threatening? Why risk their business? Unless the guy wasn't a stalker. Maybe Lovey owed him money.

Not many people were shopping in this touristy area so early. A few shops showed signs of getting ready for the business day. Interior lights winked on, but "closed" signs remained illuminated. Thorne found a parking space conveniently angled to watch Foxglove's lair.

The name of the business matched the flyer in Lovey's cottage. Demetrius Foxglove's Love Parlor and Sir Lancelot's Videography Services. The police should be all over a place like this, but it appeared to have been in business for several years.

Before Thorne devised a plan of action, the door opened, and out stepped the man himself. Demetrius Foxglove wore a designer suit. In the video, Thorne hadn't noticed that the suit looked a little frayed around the edges. The guy was handsome, for certain. Gleaming black curls were trimmed close to his scalp. His deep brown, clean-shaven complexion was flawless. His suit was clearly tailored. "Bespoke," they called it. He was too thin to buy off the rack.

He headed up the street toward a donut shop. Thorne followed. If nothing panned out in his investigation, he could replenish his supply of sweet treats. He had an extra mouth to feed, for the time being.

"Let's go, doggy." Thorne wished he knew the little animal's name. But she seemed happy enough to hang out with Thorne.

He peeked through the donut shop's large window. Foxglove was picking one of everything from the glass-fronted display cases. Thorne wondered whether the man planned to eat any of them at all. He was so skinny. But maybe he was sharing them with his castle full of princesses.

Which might include the dog's owner.

Foxglove paid for the two boxes of donuts. Thorne ducked behind a young, spindly tree. In the winter, there were no leaves to help provide camouflage. Maybe any prying eyes would focus on the pink poodle in the matching fur coat and boots, and not the man in the trench coat hiding behind the narrow tree branches.

The donut shop door opened. The sweet, yeasty scent of delicious baked goods wafted into the cold winter air. Thorne's stomach growled.

Foxglove stepped outside, balancing the boxes on his arms.

The poodle barked. Not with one of her delicate little yips. She tugged on the pink leash, lunging at Foxglove.

The dog really didn't like this guy. Or maybe she wanted a donut. Thorne couldn't decipher dog code.

Foxglove ignored Thorne entirely, watching his own feet to avoid the snarling jaws of the pink tornado. A bus wheezed to a stop at the curb. Foxglove hustled on board.

A guy with a business and a fancy suit had to ride the bus?

Thorne looked at the illuminated sign displayed above the bus windshield. The route number and destination name indicated it was headed to the main terminal downtown.

"Come on, doggy."

He lifted the poodle into his arms and jogged to his car. His trench coat was instantly soiled with wet dog prints. Thorne drove to the bus terminal. Parking downtown was a bear. By the time he found a spot and plugged a couple of quarters in the meter, the bus had come and gone.

And Thorne was out fifty cents.

# 9

# ❋ Brie ❋

Brie had survived leading the morning class of seniors. Monday's afternoon class started soon. *Two classes in one day.* Brie sighed. She couldn't bear the thought of yet another hour of humiliation as old people suggested she loosen up and act her age.

"You're twenty-five," one snide old lady had said, "not seventy-five."

*Lovey has to come back to save me from this. Time to call Dad.*

When he answered, Brie heard yipping in the background and road noises, telling her Dad still had the dog, and he was driving.

"You haven't found Lovey yet?" Brie asked her PI father on the phone.

"I'm hot on Lovey's trail. I found her stalker," Dad said.

"Stalker?" Brie asked, alarmed.

"Yeah, didn't I tell you about him already?"

"Absolutely not!"

"Oh." Dad sounded nonchalant. "I think her stalker has been in her cottage pretending to be her dog-sitter."

"This is creepy!" Brie exclaimed. "We need to tell the police."

"Not yet. I've almost cracked this case."

"Lovey could be in danger, and you want to slow down the investigation for your pride?" Brie wouldn't wait for her father to do the right thing. She'd most certainly inform real authorities about this development as soon as she got off the phone with her father. *I have to tell Riggs.* She tried to convince herself she wasn't casting about for an excuse to talk to Officer Saito. "The first twenty-four hours of a case are the most critical."

"You make me sound like a monster. I'm doing this investigation for free. And I'm making progress. Do you really want to involve the police before we know for certain that Lovey's in danger? How embarrassing would it be for a SWAT team to swoop in and grab her at that romance convention if nothing's wrong?" Dad paused, and Brie heard another "yip" in the background. "We need to know more before we call in the authorities."

The road noise got louder.

"Dad, I can barely hear you."

"I had to roll the windows down the rest of the way," her father said. "This dog is really smelly."

"What did you do to that poor poodle?" Brie asked with dread.

She didn't have a lot of pets growing up, and when she did, her father was ordered to keep completely hands off. The one dog she had as a child nearly died when her father had fed him all the dark chocolates from a variety box because "nobody else in this house will eat them."

"Remember, dogs can't eat chocolate."

"Right. I'll never forget *that* bill. The dog is fine. I gave her Angus Assistant for dinner last night. Is pink really a natural fur color for dogs?"

"I don't think so." Brie rolled her eyes. *Angus Assistant?* Her father was hopeless. But at least it wasn't chocolate. An alarm on her phone pinged. *Time for dance class.* Reporting Lovey's disappearance to the police might be premature. Maybe her increasing feeling of concern was influenced by her love of true crime podcasts. And her interest in the handsome policeman. "I've gotta go."

"Wait, I have more to discuss with you. Can you meet me at The Celery Maiden for a healing brew later? Say maybe, one-ish?"

"Can it wait until after work? I have a real job," Brie said. *Unlike someone I know.*

"Oh, right," Dad said. "I guess that's okay."

"Fine. Talk to you later."

"Bye Cheeser," Dad said, using one of the nicknames Brie loathed.

Brie hung up. If her father's report wasn't reassuring, Brie would call the police about Lovey. But right now, if she didn't get to the dance class on time, there would be Brie's homicide to report. She suspected the seniors weren't actually learning anything from her. They were simply entertaining themselves by watching Brie's failures.

Brie stepped through the door to the dance room and saw Riggs already inside, twerking with expert skill. Officer Riggs Saito wasn't wearing his uniform today. Instead, he had donned workout clothes of loose track pants that flattered his lean, long legs. A skintight black shirt hugged every ripple of his chiseled upper body. His usually stiff black hair wasn't slicked back today. Instead, it fell in gentle waves across the top of his head. His square jaw was set in a smile that caused dimples to—

"You okay there, Brie?" Sam Slate waved a hand in front of Brie's face.

"She's just stoned, as usual." George Saito, Riggs's grandfather, stood in front of his rollator with his arms crossed over his narrow chest. "This is the kind of place my ungrateful grandson sentenced me to. I might as well be in jail, with all the hoodlums and dopeheads."

"Oh!" *Yikes, I did it again.* Brie tore her attention from Rigg's ripped abs to the cranky seniors. "Lovey still isn't back, so I'm here to teach again. And I'm not stoned!"

"*Right*," George said. "Lucky for us, my grandson showed up to teach the class today."

"Grandpa, you know I can only stay for a few minutes," Riggs explained. "I'm here to take you to your doctor's appointment."

"We can be late. The doctor will be."

The other seniors all frowned and nodded in agreement.

"Officer Saito," Brie said nervously.

"Please. You know it's Riggs."

"Riggs." Brie smiled. He had apparently forgiven her for her last run-in with the law. Her resolve to wait until after talking to her father dissolved in the glow of the officer's smile. "We need to file a missing person's report."

"For Lovey?" The cookie lady looked concerned.

"Now hold on there," Diana Diamond said. "I don't think she'd want us getting Johnny Law involved. What with her past and all."

"Her past?" Brie asked. "What's so bad about being a cable TV star?"

"Years before she was on television, she was a real Las Vegas showgirl," Sam said. "Quite well-known, in her day."

"Wow! That's cool." Brie still wasn't getting it. "But, why would that make Lovey afraid of the police?"

"So Las Vegas is full of gangsters. What if someone from the mob is after her?" Diana suggested.

Brie quirked an eyebrow. "The mob? Really?" She'd only seen stuff like that in old movies. None of her favorite true crime podcasts talked about the mob. "Is the mafia still a thing?"

"Actually, it is," Riggs said. "It's just different than what you see in movies nowadays. It's never a bad idea to get the police involved. I can—" Riggs started.

"Hush, boy," George whispered loudly. "They have a good point."

"Why don't we officially hire your father, the private

investigator, to do the job?" the cookie lady asked Brie.

Brie asked, "Like, for money?"

"How much does he charge?" Layton asked.

Brie had no idea, but her father always seemed to be on the knife-edge of being broke.

Before she could offer an estimate, Sam spoke up. "I'm on a fixed income. I don't have a lot to spare."

The others grumbled similar sentiments.

"Do you think he would do it in exchange for treats?" the cookie lady suggested. "He loves my cooking. Especially my new recipe for peanut brittle."

"You want to pay my father candy to find Lovey?" Brie was momentarily horrified, but then she considered her father's raging sweet tooth. "That just might work."

"Hey, I don't like the idea of putting something so serious into the hands of a civilian in exchange for peanut brittle." Riggs put his hands on his narrow hips. "I must insist on—"

"You're not on duty," George interrupted. "The Las Vegas mafia is no joke. I don't care for PIs either, but we need to protect this lady. I'd much rather Thorne be in the front line of danger."

"Wait, what?" Brie asked. Everyone ignored her.

"Fine," Riggs said. "But I'll do everything I can for Lovey without turning this into an official investigation. It's the right thing to do." Riggs glanced at his smart watch. "We're out of time here. Come on, Grandpa."

The two left for George's appointment. Brie went to work dancing, trying to put the troubling scenario presented by the seniors far from her mind.

*Las Vegas gangsters?* There had to be a true crime podcast about the mob. She'd find it later and do her own research. *This case might be out of Dad's league.*

# 10

# ✳ Thorne ✳

"Hey, Thorne!" The owner of The Celery Maiden Healing Brews greeted him with a cheerful smile. Several children dashed around serving beverages to patrons. The hippie family running the place always seemed to be in a good mood.

*Maybe it's because they drink their own spring water concoctions.*

"The usual?" Jade Grassley asked. His dark hair was twined into dozens of narrow dreadlocks, tied in a bun sort of deal on top of his head.

*Not dreadlocks.* Brie was trying to break Thorne of using the "outdated and offensive" name for the natural hairstyle. "There's nothing dreadful about them," Brie had told Thorne. "They're just locs."

Jade wiped a clean towel across the bar top of the sunny atrium shop. There was no alcohol served at this bar, which suited Thorne fine.

"I'll have a celery juice," he said. "But I need something special for my daughter. What's a good drink for a girl?"

"Brie is coming?" Phoebe asked. Jade's pale blond wife waved from her station behind a juicer.

Thorne nodded.

"I'd say the Moon Goddess brew." She described the

special health benefits of the concoction for women to Thorne.

The poodle yipped.

"You brought a friend today," Jade said.

"I'm dog-sitting," Thorne explained.

"That looks just like Lovey's dog," Phoebe said.

"Have you seen Lovey?" Thorne asked.

"Not since last week. But she doesn't come in very often," Jade said.

"Well, if she comes around, let me know. Do you still have my business card that I gave you last month?"

"Sure do!" Jade replied.

Thorne used some of his earnings from the insurance case to purchase the celery juice for himself and the special woman juice for Brie. He grabbed the juices with their paper straws, napkins, and an extra cup. He found a table.

"Yip!"

"Hush, doggy." Thorne filled the extra cup with celery juice and set it on the tabletop for the yipping pink poodle. Maybe the juice would help her with her horrific gas.

He would hate for anything to mar his visit with Brie. Finally, the daddy-daughter bonding time Thorne had seen so much of in movies was happening in his own life. Thorne was pleasantly surprised that she agreed to meet with him. It was a good sign for their relationship.

Thorne felt healthier just being inside the juice joint. He had already blown the diet Barry put him on. He suspected his friend would say Angus Assistant wasn't that great of a dinner choice. *Too many carbs. Not to mention the sodium and MSG.* New Year's resolution number one wasn't going all that well.

*It doesn't matter! I'm doing the right thing now. Nothing but celery juice for the rest of the day.*

"Hi, Dad," Brie came to his table. She was carrying a small flat box.

"Yip Yip!" The poodle walked in circles on top of the table. She looked a little dirty. The dog had gotten gray snow-slush on her coat during their donut shop surveillance.

"Cheesy Briesy!" Thorne stood to give her a hug. She let him, though the whole thing felt stiff. "This is wonderful!"

They sat down. Brie set the box on the table. The dog sniffed it and barked.

"I got you this juice," Thorne said. "I think you'll really like it."

"Uh, thanks." Brie took a tiny sip and made a sour face. "What . . . is this?"

"It's cranberry-beet juice. It's great for the digestion and urinary tract. It's supposed to be really good for women. They usually include apple juice to sweeten it, but the added sugar isn't good for you."

"How . . . considerate," Brie said.

She took another sip and grimaced. *She doesn't like it?* Then she sort of smiled and nodded before setting it on the table.

"Thanks, Dad," Brie said. "It tastes so . . . healthy."

Thorne felt relieved. The dog went right for Brie's juice and sniffed at the cup. Brie lifted it out of harm's way. Then the animal went back to the box and scratched at it with her paws.

"Does the dog have to be on the table?"

"Um, I guess not. Come on, dog." Thorne lifted the pup.

He didn't think he squeezed the doggy, but a noxious cloud erupted from her. Brie gagged.

"Is that smell coming from the poodle?" she asked, holding a paper napkin over her nose.

"The dog seems to have digestive issues," Thorne said. "I don't know how Lovey stands the smell."

"Wait, you're still calling her 'dog?'" Brie exclaimed. "As a PI, shouldn't you be able to figure out her name?"

"It's a minor mystery," Thorne said.

Brie sighed and reached under the dog's neck.

"You need to see the jewelry?" Thorne asked. "It wears some kind of necklace under this red flower. It's a fancy dog."

"Those are her dog tags," Brie said, moving the red flower

decoration to one side.

"Isn't that a military thing?" Thorne asked.

Brie rolled her eyes.

"Hey, I saw that," Thorne said.

"Look, Dad." Brie turned the tag to Thorne's face. "Her name is Duchess."

"Oh." Thorne winced. *Her name was right there all along?* He set Duchess on the floor with her celery juice.

Brie looked around The Celery Maiden before leaning in to whisper. "I'm actually glad you invited me to meet in person in case our phones are tapped."

"Why, what's going on?"

"Lovey might have been involved in the mob," Brie explained.

"I didn't see anything mafia-related in her apartment," Thorne said. "Although there's no reason her stalker couldn't be part of the mob. He wears a pretty slick suit, after all."

"Mobsters need frontmen to interact with law-abiding society," Brie said. "I found a true crime podcast that's all about mafia cases. For research, you know."

Thorne nodded and grinned. Brie was a chip off the old block with her budding interests.

Brie continued, "Mafias mean business! They mostly do so-called white-collar crime these days. Hacking, money laundering, scams. And sometimes the police are in on their crimes. We can't trust anyone. Did you know there's a mafia in Pueblo?"

"I've heard that," Thorne said. Pueblo was a little more than a half hour's drive from Colorado Springs. The mob had been a big deal in the past. Now, the pretty city was more famous for its reservoir and river walk. They also hosted the state fair every summer. *How far could Foxglove have taken Lovey? Does the bus run to Pueblo?* "Are you saying Lovey's in Pueblo?"

"Dad! No!" Brie glanced around the busy juice bar, then lowered her voice. "You told me you've almost cracked the case.

I thought that meant you'd figured out where she is."

"I have a hot lead," Thorne said. "I'm doing this for free. I've already burned up a half a tank of gas tailing a suspect. I'd love to continue investigating, but I need to find another job that pays actual money." His last missing senior case had only resulted in two celery juices. "If the mob is involved, why haven't Lovey's friends called the police?"

"Because it's too dangerous!" Brie said frantically. She looked around again and whispered, "Even George Saito warned Officer Riggs to stay away from the case."

The "incomparable" retired detective Saito was afraid of the mob? Thorne smirked. PIs like Thorne were at a distinct advantage here. They could work around the law to get the job done.

Brie leaned back and said, "This job may not pay money." Brie passed the box she brought with her across the table to Thorne. "But it does pay." She tapped a finger on the box lid. "Open it."

Curious, Thorne lifted the lid. "Oh no!" He shut it fast. Then he lifted it again, slowly. "Gee, Brie, there must be two pounds of peanut brittle in here."

"The cookie lady made this batch especially for you," Brie explained.

"So it's *that* brittle." Thorne's heart started palpitating. He took a sip of his celery juice in an attempt to wash away the saliva that had gathered there, thinking about the delicious treat. *What about my diet?* "The cookie lady's peanut brittle . . . Hey. Do you know that woman's name?"

Brie shook her head and shrugged.

"I'm in." Thorne snatched a tile of the brittle from the box and nibbled a crisp, flaky chunk into his mouth. "But I need your help."

He slid the key to Lovey's cottage across the table and kept it under his hand. Brie took the hint and laid her hand over his. Thorne pulled his hand back, and Brie slid the key to herself.

"What's this for?" Brie asked.

"Cottage 1. I need you to hold on to this key just in case something happens to me. I have to catch a fox."

"Didn't you say Lovey's stalker was hanging around her cottage?" Brie asked.

"Not with Thorne Bramble on the case. I'll be on him like milk stains on baby clothes.

"Okay . . . Before you become a milk stain, do you mind coming with me to Lovey's place?" Brie said. "I'll get some real dog food from Lovey's for Duchess."

"Dog food? Duchess doesn't want that. I have the food situation covered." At Brie's disappointed expression, he added, "We can bring the kibble to my townhouse later. You can stay for dinner. I cook a mean Angus Assistant!" He glanced down at the poodle. "Don't I?"

The dog looked up at Thorne, wrinkling its cute black nose.

"No thanks, Dad. And I'm keeping Duchess with me so you don't do permanent damage to the poor thing."

Thorne wanted to protest. He was becoming fond of the pink poodle. Until another noxious cloud filled his tortured sinuses.

# 11

# ❋ Lovey ❋

Lovey folded her arms across the front of the white satin leotard spelling out "dance" in sparkling dark pink letters. The walk-in closet full of delightful dancewear had been too much of a temptation to resist. It nearly rivaled Sam Slate's room full of elaborate costuming supplies. The kicky skirts, the strappy dance heels. The feather boas in all the colors of the rainbow.

*A girl could get used to dressing like this.*

But giving up her puppy was a bridge too far to cross.

By Monday afternoon, the ninja still hadn't delivered Duchess to the Hoffman home. Lovey was getting seriously annoyed. And frantic. When Lovey demanded answers, Harry and Sally insisted the ninja would make good on her word.

"She doesn't lie. It isn't the ninja's way," Harry insisted. He wiped down the glass top of the stove in the modest kitchen.

"I'm sure she's doing everything in her power to find Duchess, Mom," Sally said. She sat on a stool with her laptop resting on the tall counter in front of her.

"This is just a little hiccup. In the meantime, what do you think about signing the contract?" Harry asked.

"This is extortion," Lovey said. "Withholding my precious Duchess, forcing me to sign a contract that can't possibly be legally binding."

The contract was a roll of rice paper parchment. Lovey was supposed to sign it with a long black raven's feather. A small pot of ink engraved with a Yin and Yang symbol sat next to the quill. The implements contrasted dramatically with the bright, cozy yellow kitchen.

Lovey steamed with anger. Her hope to escape while the children were in school that day was foiled by the Hoffmans. They didn't work remotely every day, but both made sure to arrange their schedules to act as prison guards. That's not how the cheerful couple described it, but Lovey felt trapped.

"But Mom—" Harry started.

"I'm nobody's mother," Lovey huffed.

Harry and Salley looked crestfallen.

"I have limited resources," Lovey continued. "I have barely enough to support myself. If you were hoping to lure me into leaving you a vast estate, then bumping me off—"

"Good heavens, no!" Sally exclaimed.

"We don't want your money," Harry said. "Money is completely irrelevant."

Both husband and wife looked horrified. The reaction appeared genuine. A lifetime in the performing arts had made Lovey a good judge of whether a person was putting on an act.

Lovey's investment portfolio was adequate to support her current lifestyle. The cottage at Hummingbird Gardens wasn't cheap. Her only hope was that the two ex-husbands mooching off her with their ridiculous claims for alimony would croak before she did.

*Bad choices with worse consequences.*

"We aren't exactly rolling in the dough," Harry said, "but Sally and I both have careers. I'm a receptionist at an insurance office."

"And I work in a department store," Sally said. "I'm a manager. One of a team." She shrugged. "It's not much, but it's a living."

"Why do you want me around?" Lovey asked. "Another

mouth to feed. If you didn't kidnap me for money, then I'm just a liability."

"Contrary to the song in Cabaret," Sally said, "money does not make the world go around. The reason we want to adopt you into our family has nothing to do with finances."

"We're hardworking people," Harry said. He reached for Sally's hand. "Our early life choices put us at a disadvantage in the job market. Both of us majored in film and theater."

"We met in college," Sally said. "We had big dreams."

"Big," Harry said, nodding.

"But we're realistic, too. We married and started a family, and set those dreams aside, for the most part."

"We still audition for local theater roles," Harry said. "Even apply for stage theater manager positions. Anything to be in that world."

"We've gotten all the way to the job interview stage," Sally said sadly, "but we never seem to get the job."

"Or the big stage roles," Harry said. "Supporting characters, but never the leading man or lady."

Lovey brushed her hands through her silver waves. "I still don't understand. What does any of this have to do with me?"

"You lived your dreams," Sally said. "I'm proud of what we've built, as a family. Our home. Our kids. But if you become our mother, the kids will see how following their dreams is just as valid a life choice as following a career just to pay the bills."

"Don't you have examples in your own family?" Lovey asked. "Parents? Grandparents?"

"Neither of us has living grandparents," Harry said. "My dad is only interested in his career as a proctologist in Massachusetts. We hardly ever see him. And my mom is too busy running her charity, Saint Fiacre's Hemorrhoid Healing Solutions, to be a grandmother."

*It sounds like Harry's parents both have their heads up their own—*

Sally interrupted Lovey's train of thought. "My father died

of a heart attack at his desk at work," Sally said. "My mother remarried a pastry chef and moved to Lichtenstein."

"None of our parents encouraged our theater dreams," Harry said. "Maybe we would have had the courage to take the risk if they had. Instead, we've got these pay-the-bills jobs."

"We perform whenever we get the chance," Sally said. "Like the Valentine's Showcase. It's at Randy's school theater at Juniper Breeze High School. These little events are the only way we can keep a fragment of our old dream alive."

Lovey managed to keep her expression neutral, but her brain screamed "Showcase!" Her HMCA students would be performing at the same high school. Escape, or rescue, was within reach. While her thoughts reeled, the couple continued their story of lost dreams.

"I missed out on having a real relationship with my parents. And the kids need guidance from your generation," Harry added. "I mean, look at Randy—"

"What about me? It's Randall, by the way." The teen wearing the thigh-high black platform boots clomped into the room. "What are you guys talking about?"

"Don't sneak up on us like that, dear," Sally said.

"I'm home from school," Randall said. "Like I always am at this time of day. Unfortunately, this is where I live." He turned and nodded toward Lovey. "Hi, old lady."

"Watch your tone, young man." Harry frowned.

Chrissy raced in behind Randall. She slammed into Lovey with a hug.

"Grandma! I've been thinking about you all day! I'm so glad we're finally together again! I have so much to tell you about school."

"First things first, Chrissy," Sally said. "Kids, hang up your coats. Do you have any homework?"

"I didn't wear a coat today. And I already did all my work in class," Randall said. He opened the refrigerator and started poking around.

"I have a little homework." Chrissy wrinkled her nose. "But I can do it later."

"A stitch in time saves nine," Harry said.

"I bet I can make your homework more fun." Sally grinned. She reached into a cabinet and pulled out a box of brownie mix.

"Whoa, really?" Chrissy said.

Sally nodded.

"Thanks mom!" Chrissy exclaimed. "I'll get my work done faster than you can say 'supercalifragilisticexpialidocious'!"

Chrissy hung her coat up and started her homework while Harry helped Sally make the brownies. The little girl and her parents were almost a caricature of cheerful musical comedy actors. Ever bright and optimistic. Under different circumstances, they would be the perfect family for Lovey. The family she never had.

But not at the expense of her freedom and autonomy.

"Want to help us make brownies, Mom?" Sally asked.

"If that will grant me my freedom," Lovey said.

"The old lady's feisty," Randall said. "Maybe we should keep her around after Mom and Dad are thrown in jail for kidnapping. Especially if something bad happens to the dog."

Lovey placed a hand against her chest, certain those very words had just caused her heart to burst.

"Oh! I feel faint!"

Sally threw an arm around her shoulders and guided her to the frilly bedroom Lovey had come to appreciate.

"You'd better lie down," Sally said. "Catch your breath." Lovey reclined into the soft pillows. Sally pulled a knitted pink blanket over her. "After a little rest, you'll feel right as rain."

She threw one arm across her eyes as she waited for Sally to leave. Alone with her thoughts, Lovey scrambled for a solution.

*How am I going to get out of this?*

The door creaked open, then clicked closed. She lowered her arm. Randall drifted to her bedside. His black clothing and spikey boots were probably supposed to make him look dangerous. But his eyeliner emphasized his large eyes, adding a touch of innocence to his young face.

"Have you come to stab me in the heart again?" Lovey asked.

The kid chuckled. A sound Lovey hadn't expected to come from the serious teen. "For a fluffy old lady, you can be really dark. No. I came to apologize. That ninja lady isn't evil. There's no way she would hurt your dog."

Lovey rolled on her side and patted the pink bedspread. Randall perched on the edge of the bed beside Lovey.

"I have a feeling neither of us fits in here," Lovey said. "Not completely. What's your story?"

"My story?" Randall asked.

"Surrounded by all this cheerfulness, you choose to be, what is it called? Goth?"

"I'm more alternative than anything. But I'm not really into labels."

*Alternative to what? The kid looks goth to me.*

Randall threw his arms up. "I just can't take it sometimes, you know? I mean, life's not really like this. The bright colors. The smiles. Everything ending up all right."

"I understand."

"How can you?" Randall asked. "You're like my parents. Like Chrissy. All pink and lacey and happy."

"Randall. Sometimes the people who seem the most cheerful are hiding the biggest wounds."

That seemed to make him hit the pause button on his pity party for a moment. When he spoke again, his words were less strident.

"Well, I don't like pretending. I mean, I like acting. That's kind of my thing. But in real life, I want to be who I really am. And that's not always happy."

"Wise words for such a young man." Lovey smiled with pride. Though she wasn't sure where that emotion came from. It wasn't like Randall was her real grandson.

"If I tell you something, do you promise not to tell my parents?"

"No, Randall, I can't do that," Lovey said sternly. "If you're participating in dangerous activities—"

"Dude! It's nothing like that," Randall said. His pale complexion, lightly marred with a few spots of acne, flamed pink with a blush. "It's just embarrassing."

"Oh." Lovey was quiet for a moment. The boy was giving her his trust. It touched her heart. If he were engaged in some truly unhealthy behavior, she might be forced to break the promise. Shatter this tiny shred of connection with the teen. This small crack in the boy's crusty exterior deserved exploration, at least. "I . . . I promise to keep your secret."

He sat up straight on his bedside perch, a smile cracking his dreary façade. "I got the lead role in my high school skit based on *The Tell-Tale Heart*," Randall said proudly.

"That's incredible, Randall! Why won't you tell your parents?" Lovey asked, relief flooding her. "They'd be so proud—"

"No. They wouldn't." Randall squeezed his hand into a fist. "You've seen how they are. Edgar Allen Poe? They'd be horrified, not happy for me."

Lovey had to admit he might be right. "They may take a little time to get there, but they'll come around eventually."

"I hate lying to them. Most of our rehearsals have been during the lunch hour, but I had to stay late after school a few times. I told Dad and Mom I've been getting tutoring for my math class when I've really been working on the skit. It was a dumb lie, because I'm really not good at math. I actually do need tutoring. My grade keeps going down, and my parents are like, 'What's wrong with this tutor?' It sucks."

"Language, young man," Lovey scolded.

"Seriously?" He shook his head. "It's not like I'll keep it on cap forever." Randall must have noticed Lovey's confused expression. He added, "On cap. You know, secret."

"Ah," Lovey said.

Randall continued, "They're gonna find out. The high school theater group is performing the skit as part of the Valentine's Showcase. I just don't want to deal with my parents judging me right now."

Randall let his chin drop to his chest dramatically, as though the weight of the world rested on his teenage head. A head with poorly dyed black hair. His blond roots showed prominently in large, blotchy patches. It was ruining the aesthetic.

"Who does your hair?" Lovey asked.

"I do." He brushed his fingers through the shaggy locks. "Mom and Dad won't let me get it professionally done. And my Grandpa Hoffman says I'll never get into medical school wearing all black, 'cause patients don't trust doctors unless they wear white jackets. But I don't even want to be a doctor. Especially not a butt doctor."

Lovey couldn't stop a giggle, although she was certain that encouraging that sort of attitude would win her no favors with Randall's parents. *Who cares about what a couple of kidnappers think?*

Lovey quirked an eyebrow at Randall. "Do you have any more dye?"

# 12

# ❊ Brie ❊

*And this is how I'm spending my Monday evening.* Brie tiptoed through the freezing cold behind her father toward Lovey's cottage with Duchess in her arms.

"Stealth is an artform. Paint the sidewalk with your footsteps. Mold your body into the shadows, like clay," Dad said quietly. He slid his feet like a Fremen across the Dune planet, Arrakis.

He didn't look very stealthy with the coil of rope he had dangling from his arm, and the roll of duct tape he wore as a bracelet.

"If the stalker is at the cottage, shouldn't we be making noise to scare him off?" Brie asked.

"You said it, yourself: the police could be in on this if this guy is from the mafia. The only way to catch this monster is to get him ourselves."

Brie regretted implicating the police. *I mean, we're talking about the Colorado Springs Police Department.* The thought of beloved local law enforcement being tangled up with organized crime seemed silly.

Her father apparently thought they could take a mobster down by sneaking up on him. Despite Brie's reminders that real life wasn't a video game, Dad was confident in his plan. Brie's hopes rested on either Lovey being home, or nobody else showing up. But everything she'd ever learned from true crime podcasts said that she was walking into a death trap.

Duchess wriggled in Brie's arms. Despite her coat and boots, the pup shivered like she was cold.

Brie stopped in her tracks. "Dad, let's go. I can just buy some dog food. I'm sure Duchess will be—"

"Hush!" Dad grabbed Brie's arm and tugged her behind a large evergreen near the sidewalk. He whispered, "Someone's coming."

Brie peeked from behind the tree. A large man with light steps walked up the path. Brie recognized him immediately.

"That's just Layton Lambert," Brie whispered. "He lives in one of the cottages."

Dad held a finger to his lips. Brie rolled her eyes and stayed quiet until Layton passed.

Dad finally stepped back onto the sidewalk. "He didn't see us. Good job being quiet, Brie." He nodded toward the dog, "And you, too, Duchess. That man could have compromised our mission. We couldn't let him see us like this." Dad lifted the rope.

"No, I suppose we couldn't. Let's just get this over with."

Dad's exaggerated tiptoeing, combined with his ridiculous PI costume reminded Brie of the spy from vintage Pink Panther cartoons she had seen online.

When they finally made it to Lovey's cottage, Dad shoved his gear into Brie's arms, while she reluctantly handed over the poodle.

"What even is this for?" Brie asked, grasping the heavy silver roll of tape and the coarse sisal rope.

"To immobilize the intruder. Tie him up."

"Okay, but the duct tape?"

"In case he tries to scream for help," Dad said. "Do you have your pepper spray handy?"

"It's in my purse," Brie said, "which I can't get into now,

because I'm carrying your kidnapping supplies. Why do you get to carry the dog?" The poodle was lighter than the coils of rope. There was enough to tie up an elephant.

"She's just like Lassie," Dad said. "She can tell us if someone's here. First, me and Duchess will check the perimeter."

*Who the heck is Lassie?* Brie decided not to ask, lest her father's answer make this whole ordeal take even longer. She could Google it later.

Brie shifted the rope so she could reach into her coat pocket one-handed. *Don't drop it!* A dunking in the slushy snow might ruin her smartphone. Brie clicked on her phone flashlight, shining it on the snowy ground along the front border of Lovey's cottage.

"There are no footprints," Brie said. "I don't think you need to—"

"Haven't you ever read any Sir Arthur Conan Doyle? Footprints mean nothing when devious criminals are involved. Wait here while we circle the place." Dad disappeared around a corner of the cottage with the poodle in his arms.

*There are footprints now.* Brie shook her head at the sight of the obvious prints left by Dad's clunky, old-fashioned dress shoes.

Brie stood on the front porch for a few moments, shivering, weighed down by the rope and duct tape her father saddled her with. She started to Google who Lassie might be, but stopped when movement caught her eye.

The figure was much too small to be Layton. Or any man she knew, for that matter. And they were dressed in all black.

*The ninja!*

Brie took a step toward her, but then she was gone. *Where did she go?* Before Brie could go after her, Dad came from behind the cottage.

"Duchess is giving the all clear," Dad said. "Plus, she took care of business. Two birds with one stone. She's an efficient doggy."

"Quiet," Brie whispered. "I just saw the ninja."

Dad's head turned on a swivel. "Where?"

"I don't know. She just disappeared," Brie said.

Her father looked at her skeptically.

"Why would I lie about this?" Brie frowned.

"About *this*, specifically? Why would you lie to your dad at all?"

"Ugh!" Brie slammed the rope and tape onto the porch step and pulled out the key her father had given her. She unlocked the door. "Come on."

"Wait!" Dad whispered. He held Duchess with one arm and pulled a canister from the pocket of his brown trench coat with his free hand. A brand-new set of paw prints tracked across the fabric of Dad's coat.

"Yip." Duchess barked quietly.

"Duchess says it's safe, but we shouldn't go inside unarmed. There could be a trap. Get out your pepper spray."

"What? No!" Brie took a step back. She had bad memories of the noxious stuff.

"These brand-new ones are fresh, so they'll spray in a stream instead of clouding up an entire area," Dad said.

Brie took the pink canister from her purse, and Dad pulled out one of his own, in a shiny black color.

"You'll be my backup," Dad continued. "Be ready to spring on the stalker and tie him up."

"Why me?" Brie exclaimed.

"While I spray him and keep him distracted, you can come up from behind and—"

Tired of her father's nonsense, Brie reached around the doorframe and flipped the living room light switch on.

"What are you doing?" Dad whispered loudly, flicking the switch off.

"Looking for traps and stalkers and mobsters and ninjas," Brie said in a rush. "Wouldn't it be easier to find them with the lights on?"

"You're ruining our element of surprise. Just use your phone light."

Brie didn't think beams from her phone would be any less surprising, but she complied. She was done arguing with her father. She just wanted to go home.

Dad secured the living room, then he escorted Brie and Duchess to the dark kitchen. Brie set Duchess down, and the pup immediately dashed to her full kibble dish and feasted, crunching loudly. Brie bumbled around with her phone light, looking for dog supplies.

She found a canvas tote bag covered with a rainbow of colored paw prints, and packed a few cans of dog food, and the bag of Delicate Tummy Gourmet Crumbles dog kibble.

While she packed, Dad jumped and rolled from room to room with his pepper spray, tripping now and then when his feet got tangled up in his trench coat.

After Duchess finished eating, Brie picked the pup up. "Dad, it's time to go."

Dad panted as he walked into the kitchen. His face was covered in sweat. "If anyone from the mob is here, he's hiding real good."

"Yip!" Duchess seemed to agree.

"I don't think we're catching any mobsters tonight," Brie said. *Or ninjas.*

*And we still haven't heard from Lovey.*

# 13

# ✳ Thorne ✳

Thorne's townhouse felt a little empty Monday night. Not as smelly, though, after Brie had insisted on taking Lovey's poodle with her. Thorne had been insulted that his daughter didn't think he knew how to feed the doggy. *Duchess.*

He scooped up another bite of leftover Angus Assistant. The noodle dish never gave *him* gas.

Pulling the fork from his mouth in preparation for shoveling up another bite, he remembered his earlier vow to only have celery juice the rest of the evening. He'd already eaten half a pound of peanut brittle. *Oh well. Too late now.*

Besides, he had burned a million calories at Lovey's cottage this evening. And he required sustenance to continue his research. Demetrius Foxglove left a huge online footprint. Thorne needed to earn his peanut brittle. Studying Foxglove's video tutorials could lead him right to Lovey.

He grimaced, imagining the sexy old lady being the love-slave of greasy Foxglove. The guy was young enough to be her grandson. Thorne focused on his laptop screen with increased determination.

The bold, manly font on Foxglove's website read, "Greetings, all you lonely incels out there."

*What is that?* Thorne did a quick search. An incel was

someone who was involuntarily celibate. The guy who had tried to seduce his daughter back in January had Foxglove's tutorials on his laptop. *Marty is an incel?* Thorne chuckled.

Then he frowned. If not for his fatherly interruption of their date, innocent young Brie might have been led astray by Marty. Because of this Foxglove guy.

*Demetrius Foxglove is a menace to decent society.*

Thorne played one of Foxglove's video tutorials.

"If you want to fill your castle with princesses," Foxglove said, "you need to look like a prince."

He yanked up his shirt, exposing six-pack abs. Those weren't the muscles Thorne expected to see after watching the skinny guy on the street outside a donut shop this morning.

"Not everyone has the time to achieve this level of fitness in a gym," Foxglove said. "That's why I offer my Demetrius Foxglove-branded airbrush kit. For merely five low payments of $19.99, you can give yourself stunning abs like mine."

He demonstrated on an artist's canvas, spraying the illusion of muscles from a pencil-looking thing connected to a slender hose onto the drawing of a man. *This Foxglove guy is a sleazy, deceptive jerk!* Thorne favorited the website address for ordering the kit. *For research purposes.*

"I know some of you out there are purists," Foxglove continued. "For these folks, I highly recommend getting six-pack abs the old-fashioned way. By working out. Martial arts are an excellent way to achieve a manly physique. Check out the abs on Tommy Tigerclaw!"

The video cut to a poorly recorded snippet of an old martial arts movie. Tommy Tigerclaw was as ripped as any bodybuilder, but in a lean, wiry way.

Foxglove offered a link to the entire movie. Thorne eagerly clicked on *He Who Follows the Shogun*. Thorne could use any help he could get, even though Barry Strong was working him like a rented mule at the gym. Thorne suspected the grainy film had been pirated long ago. He hunched over, pushing his face close to the screen in an effort to see the 1980s movie better.

The Tigerclaw guy was performing some impressive moves. He wore clothes that were more appropriate for a breakdancer than a martial artist. But his two-toed shoes didn't match the getup. *Tabi boots. The shoes of a ninja.* This wasn't just any kind of martial art. *This is ninjitsu. What if Brie hasn't been making things up? Was there a ninja near Lovey's cottage tonight?*

Thorne didn't want to be guilty of confirmation bias. *Don't jump to conclusions.* He needed more evidence.

*Clunk!*

Thorne looked up. What was that? The townhouse settling? Something contracting from the cold night air? It wasn't Duchess. Brie had "rescued" the doggy from him, convinced the Angus Assistant was going to make the dog gassy to the point of exploding.

He tried to ignore the single unexpected sound, but Thorne trusted his gut. His PI instincts whispered that he was not alone.

Thorne wished Duchess were still with him. Dogs were good protectors. Even silly-looking pink dogs. Instead of animal defense, he had to rely on himself. Thorne picked up his pepper spray.

Stepping stealthily down the hallway, he listened for any noise. He should have silenced the computer's volume. The sounds of an epic martial arts battle echoed down the hallway. His sock foot came down on the doggy's forgotten chew toy.

"Ow!"

Thorne stumbled and fell. He landed safely and quietly in a pile of dirty laundry. Thorne was momentarily thankful he was still failing at his New Year's resolution to have a clean house. He quickly pushed himself out of the smelly pile and gasped for clean air. Hopefully, the Tommy Tigerclaw movie, with its punching and slapping sounds and dramatic music, drowned out his yelp.

Cool air brushed his stubble-covered cheeks. Thorne edged

closer to his bedroom door. His back against the wall, he twisted slightly to peer inside.

The curtains flapped. It was February in Colorado. Thorne had definitely *not* left his window open.

He ducked down and trotted into the room. After examining every possible hiding place, he closed and locked the window.

*Weird.*

Unsettled, Thorne did a thorough reconnaissance of his house, checking every window and door. Nothing had been disturbed. There were no signs that any locks had been jimmied. Thorne was ready to chalk it all up to an overactive imagination when he noticed something missing.

The dog bed. And the dog's wardrobe. *Gone!*

Thorne scratched his head. What kind of thief would break into a house and steal poodle clothes?

And how? A person would have to be extremely stealthy to escape Thorne's notice.

*A ninja could do it.*

A ninja was stealthy. That was their specialty. The Tommy Tigerclaw movie continued playing in the background. Demetrius Foxglove admired the martial arts expert. Was the skinny love pirate also into ninjitsu?

Thorne shook his head. Watching the old movie had amped up his imagination. And yet, he couldn't deny that someone had entered his townhouse.

Thorne grabbed his smartphone. *Maybe I should call the cops to report the theft.* But if he did, that Riggs Saito character might tell his cranky grandfather, retired detective George, that Thorne had been robbed of purse poodle accessories. *George already thinks I'm incompetent.* Thorne slid the phone, with its cracked screen, back into his pocket.

Maybe he could calm down with a piece of peanut brittle.

# 14

# ✳ Lovey ✳

"Now *this* is what I'm talking about!" Randall held a hand mirror to look at the back of his head. "You ate that up!"

"Ate?" Lovey felt like raising her eyebrows, but that would cause wrinkles. She hadn't eaten anything while she dyed Randall's hair.

"It means you did a great job. The vibes are vibing!"

Randall looked happier than she'd ever seen the boy, so Lovey guessed his words meant something good.

She took off the disposable latex gloves she had worn to work the black dye into Randall's hair, and stood back to admire her handywork.

Going to a beautician was a luxury she hadn't always been able to afford. During lean times, she became an expert at turning her mousy brown into honey-blond. Now that her own hair had finally turned completely white, she embraced her natural color. After all, white was called platinum blond when it was worn by younger people. Lovey still dyed Duchess's hair herself. But Lovey missed the magical process of turning human hair from one color to another.

Randall set the hand mirror down. He looked like he wanted to hug Lovey, but then he frowned and put on his tough guy act again. Hugging an old lady certainly wouldn't fit with his grim persona.

Instead, he simply said, "Thank you."

Lovey smiled. The two of them joined the rest of the family for a dinner of baked cod, mashed potatoes, and a delightful green salad with homemade croutons.

After dinner Monday night, Harry clicked on the television. The family seemed to have an endless supply of musicals and romantic comedies, old and new.

"I have a request," Lovey said.

"Anything," Sally said.

"I'd like to see *The Phantom of the Opera*."

Both parents looked aghast.

"You said you love musicals," Lovey said. "*Phantom* is one of the best musicals of all time."

"But it's so dark, Mom," Sally said. "And scary."

"Sounds great," Randall said. "I'll make the popcorn."

They weren't even halfway through when Harry admitted the songs were pretty good. Not anything he was interested in, he told Lovey, but he could see why it was popular. By the intermission, Lovey noticed everyone's heads bobbing to the rhythm of the music.

If only Lovey's own family had given her a chance to show them what she was passionate about. Her parents rejected her for moving to Las Vegas and becoming a showgirl. They wounded her badly by lamenting about wasting so much money on years of dance lessons, just for Lovey to become a "glorified stripper." Sadness filled her heart even now at the memory of the harsh words. Every girl on that stage was as talented as any prima ballerina. They just wore less clothing.

Lovey's parents refused to understand. They wouldn't even watch her cable TV show. And now they were gone. Tears tugged at Lovey's eyes. She grabbed a pink tissue from a box near the sofa.

"I need one, too," Sally said. "The phantom." She grabbed a tissue and dabbed her nose. "This is so sad!"

"Uncle!" Harry cried out, slapping a hand against his thigh. He yanked three tissues from the box and sobbed in earnest.

When the movie was over, the box of tissues was empty.

"I hope you don't have nightmares," Sally said to Chrissy.

"I've seen scarier shows at slumber parties," Chrissy said. "And they didn't have good music like this."

"I liked it," Randall said. "Finally, we got to watch a movie that was high key sick."

*More strange teen speak?* Randall was smiling.

"I just never imagined a dark musical would be something you'd enjoy, Lovey," Harry said, looking thoughtful.

"Your television show was so light," Sally added. "Uplifting. Cheerful."

"You can't have light without shadows," Lovey said.

Sally bit her lower lip, and Harry frowned. They looked uncomfortable. Normally, Lovey would have felt bad for stirring up such deep emotions. She cautioned herself not to feel for this family. They were kidnappers. Despite Randall's reassuring words, Lovey was concerned the ninja was a lying dog thief.

If she was going to escape this situation, Lovey needed to play the role of a lifetime. She needed to pretend she was happy.

Although she had to admit to herself that she wasn't faking all of it.

# 15

# ✳ Brie ✳

After getting home Monday night, Brie ran a little warm water in her kitchen sink, with a few drops of shampoo. She didn't dare mess up the poodle's fashionable pink fur, but her dainty feet were filthy. She sudsed and rinsed Duchess's feet and tummy.

"What did my mean old Dad do to the pretty little puppy?"

Duchess wagged the pompom puff at the tip of her tail and paddled her feet in the water. She seemed ecstatic about being bathed.

Every pet brought into Brie's childhood home had ended up being her sole responsibility. Dad clearly didn't have a clue about how to take care of animals. *Or children.*

Poor Duchess grimaced with each release of foul odor, like she was  embarrassed by her own gassy condition. Getting her on the right kibble seemed to be solving that problem.

*So far.* Brie hoped she wasn't in for another round. *Yikes!*

Dad wasn't deliberately hopeless. It was just his bumbling nature. Brie had to give him some credit. After being an absentee father for a lot of her childhood, too involved in his corporate job - or a liquor bottle - to spend time with his only child, he was trying to make amends. She wasn't certain she was ready to forgive. And certainly not to forget.

*But he's the only parent I have now. I barely even hear from*

*Mom these days.*

"And here I am again," she told Duchess. "Cleaning up another of Dad's messes. Literally."

"Yip!"

Brie had enough responsibility with her job. Now she was taking over Lovey's class. Unexpectedly caring for her poodle. She had a hard enough time living her own life, and now she was living an old Vegas showgirl's life.

Brie envied Lovey's confidence. Men seemed in awe of the senior woman.

When she was around a cute guy, Brie became tongue-tied and awkward. *Well, actually only one cute guy.*

"It shouldn't matter," she told Duchess. "Why do I end up making a fool of myself around Riggs Saito? Every time! And why does it bother me so much?"

Brie had to admit it was nice having someone to talk to for a change, even if they only answered in yips and tail wags. After drying the poodle's tummy and paws, Brie changed her into a sparkly red sweater.

"What's missing?" she asked Duchess.

The poodle picked up the red rosette in her teeth.

"That's right," Brie said, thinking of Lovey's obsession with accessorizing. She obediently clipped the decoration onto the dog's collar.

*The poodle is so much more fashionable than me.* Brie let her thoughts wander to Sam Slate's magical dressing room. *Maybe I'll get to play dress-up again sometime.* If she ever went on another date. Which was looking more doubtful with the passage of time.

*I'm only twenty-five!* Brie chided herself for being negative. She had a career. Her own car. *It's not like I'm freeloading off my parents, living in their basement, like some of the people I went to high school with.* She glanced around the spacious kitchen with just a twinge of guilt.

True, Brie still lived in her childhood home. Mom had gone

on a trip to study yoga in Tibet, and didn't seem to be in any hurry to come home. It had been four years now. But Brie's situation was different than those failure-to-launch types. Brie paid rent, which was only fair at her age. She wasn't a mooch. And having the entire house to herself was a great deal, even if it was much more space than she actually needed.

She set Duchess on the kitchen floor tiles. The poodle raced into the living room, sniffing and yipping, sinking her clean paws into the thick carpeting.

"Hey, no accidents now," Brie said. "Mom would kill me."

*If she ever returns.*

Brie took Duchess into the back yard for bodily function stuff. Then she microwaved a frozen dinner while Duchess nibbled on another helping of Delicate Tummy Gourmet Crumbles.

Brie sat down with her dinner in front of the big screen TV to watch an old romcom she had seen with her mother when she was too young to understand it. As an adult, *When Harry Met Sally* had become one of her favorite movies. But she couldn't completely enjoy it because her phone pinged every few minutes with group texts from the seniors in Lovey's dance class.

Brie wished she hadn't given them her phone number. She didn't think the Hummingbird Gardens crowd was tech-savvy enough to set up group chats, let alone use them. Many of the texts were about costumes and makeup for the show, which Sam Slate answered. Some were questions about the dance routine. None of the chatter was anything Brie could help with, but they were blowing up her phone right now.

Brie couldn't ignore it any longer. She paused her movie and scrolled through the messages. She didn't have everyone's contact saved to her phone, so most texts just had a jumble of numbers next to them instead of the name of who sent it.

"The roads will be clear enough for the van. Let's go to the high school tomorrow, as planned."

"Which school is it again?"

"Juniper Breeze."

"Sounds like our substitute teacher's name. You think that's how she spells it?"

"No, hers is like the cheese."

"Do you think Lovey will be there?"

"She'd better be. Or else."

"What's that supposed to mean?"

"Or else we're going to be the laughingstock of the whole Valentine's Showcase."

The thread went on and on. Brie just skimmed the flurry of messages until her own name caught her eye.

"Can you come, Brie?"

"Yeah, Brie! She's better than nothing."

"Barely."

Brie's nose wrinkled. That was probably George.

"We need Brie. We can't do it without her."

"You there, Brie?"

"Maybe she's in trouble. Young people never do anything without their phones."

"Or she's ignoring us."

"She's probably just getting stoned again."

*Yikes!* Brie typed frantically.

"I don't do drugs! I'm here. But I have to work all day tomorrow."

"Yip!" The dog demanded Brie's attention. She tried to rub Duchess's head, but her tongue created a wet wall between her hand and the soft fur. Brie set the dog on her lap, and she calmed down, finally letting Brie pet her.

*I can't take Duchess to work with me. Maybe I should take a sick day.*

The text stream kept flowing.

"Brie, did you even look at the practice schedule? Our designated stage time isn't until evening."

Brie scrolled up in the messages and found a blurry photo of a printed schedule. The seniors weren't practicing until 7:00

PM, after the Hoffman family at 6:00, and before the Barbara Ellis Studio of Dance at 8:00.

Brie briefly contemplated saying she had plans. *And lie to all the seniors?* There was probably a special place in Hell for people who did stuff like that. Plus, it was only an hour. *And there's no hope I'll have a date, ever again. I don't even have girlfriends to hang out with. What's wrong with me?*

Brie sighed heavily as she typed, "I'll be there." *But I refuse to ride on the Hummingbird Gardens transportation van. I'll drive myself.* Brie's Subaru was great in the snow. "I will meet you all at the theater."

It was nearly Brie's bedtime when she got everything sorted out. She no longer had enough time to finish the movie, but she still wanted to unwind. She scrolled through her streaming services for something short to watch. A true-crime docuseries caught her attention. It was broken into half-hour episodes and called, "No Boys Allowed: The Crime Spree that Rocked the Rockies."

Although Brie had never heard of it, "The No Boys Allowed Club" was a gang that apparently ruled small Colorado mountain towns in the 1970s and 1980s.

Authorities suggested the gang originated out of Colorado Springs. Most of the ladies had never been caught.

Both Diana and Sam had suggested that Lovey's disappearance was related to her decades-old involvement with organized crime in Las Vegas. Had the dance instructor's past followed her to Colorado Springs, and Hummingbird Gardens?

*Gangs and mobs are basically the same thing,* Brie reasoned. *Gangs are just a little less organized.*

Brie had heard of one of the former members who had been captured and jailed. *The Gymnast Reaper was part of a girls' mob?* Last Brie heard, the woman was up for parole in September, so she was safely in prison for now. But what about the other members? They could be out and about anywhere in Colorado. Pretending to be normal people. *Or dressing up as ninjas.*

Although they'd be somewhat geriatric by now.

By the time Brie was ready for bed, she was a mess of nerves. Every creak of the house made her jump. *Why do I do this to myself?* It didn't help that Duchess kept sitting at attention and perking her ears up, listening to noises Brie couldn't hear.

Brie sat on the edge of her mattress with the lamp on. Every shadow seemed to be moving.

"Bark! Bark!" Duchess walked in circles on the bedroom carpet. Her moist black nose twitched as she seemed to search for a scent.

"What is it, girl?"

The dog sat and panted. She looked like she was smiling.

*There's nobody in the house but us,* Brie reassured herself.

Brie hadn't seen a dog bed at Lovey's cottage. Maybe Dad had it. She offered Duchess a couple of folded blankets on the floor, but it was obvious what the dog preferred.

"Okay. You can sleep with me. Just this once."

Brie lifted Duchess into bed and cuddled the pink puppy.

*Maybe I should get a pet. It would be simpler than trying to connect with humans.*

Brie reluctantly turned the lamp off. She had to get some rest. She drifted to sleep with the hundred worries and questions playing through her mind gradually subsiding. She was dreaming about pink clouds and wagging tails when Duchess growled.

"Huh?" Brie opened her eyes, totally fogged out.

The toy poodle stood on Brie's pillow, her curly pink fur tickling the side of Brie's face. Only a sliver of moonlight seeped under the bottom of the blinds. The room was too dark. She sat up and groped for the new container of pepper spray her father insisted on giving her. But it was in her purse. In the other room.

*Classic mistake.* True crime podcasts should have convinced Brie by now to keep protection close at hand.

A shadow fell across her bed. Duchess snarled.

Brie screamed with the caliber of a horror movie actress and leapt from the mattress, landing on her bare feet on the soft carpet.

*Attack! Defend!* She reached for the lamp next to her bed. *I'll smash it into his head.* But before she could grab it, a loop of rope dropped over her and wrapped around her waist, locking Brie's arms to her sides. Brie tried to scream again, but a silky cloth covered her mouth. She fell onto her back on the mattress. Images conjured by all the true crime podcasts and documentaries she'd ever seen flitted through her panicked mind.

*No!*

Duchess barked so hard she nearly levitated.

"Calm down, ladies." The voice made Brie think of a female version of *The Dark Knight* Batman.

It wasn't reassuring. *Females and non-binary people can be serial killers, too.* Brie's mind scrolled through a long list of dangerous folks who didn't fit the typical masculine profile.

The dance class feared Lovey had been taken by Las Vegas mobsters, but what if this home invader was one of the women from the No Boys Allowed Club? *A local.*

"I'm only here for Duchess," the woman said.

The dog's snarling and harsh barks softened to her typical yips. Then Brie could hear her panting happily. *Not much of a guard dog.* Duchess tromped across Brie, her tiny paws squishing into Brie's tummy as she pranced toward danger. *Maybe she* is *trying to help.* But the poodle's puff-tipped tail wagged wildly.

The intruder flicked the lamp on. Brie's eyes adjusted to the sudden flood of light in the dim room. The woman was dressed all in black. A hood masked her identity like a ninja. *The* ninja who showed up when Barry was in trouble, and earlier tonight near Lovey's cottage.

Brie attempted to shout an accusation. "I've seen you before" came out as a garbled "Off eem u efur."

"If I take this gag off your mouth, do you promise not to scream?"

There was no point in yelling for help. There was too much space between houses in the neighborhood. No one had heard her first scream. They wouldn't hear her now.

Brie nodded her compliance to the ninja's demand.

"I see you have bonded with this little dog," the ninja said. "I apologize for taking her from you. Lovey will not be happy until she is reunited with her puppy."

*She knows where Lovey is?* Brie could feel her eyes growing large.

The ninja undid the gag covering Brie's mouth.

Brie worked her jaw and licked her lips a few times before asking, "Is she home? In her cottage?"

"Lovey is safe and happier than she's ever been. I cannot reveal where until my mission is complete. She has requested I bring her the dog."

Brie had first encountered the ninja last month. Barry Strong seemed happier now than Brie had ever seen him. Maybe Brie should be committed to a mental health facility, but she trusted this ninja.

She asked breathlessly, "What have you done with Lovey?"

"I only did what was necessary. Do not worry."

"You have to let her go! We need her at the HMCA. Her class is desperate for her teaching skills."

"She'll be glad to hear that." To Duchess, she spoke in a distorted-sounding baby-talk voice. "Is the pwetty wittle puppy weady to see Lovey?"

The ninja picked up the dog. The red rosette on Duchess's collar bobbed as she frantically licked at the ninja's mask.

A puff of smoke enveloped Duchess and the woman.

"Wait! Duchess needs special food!" Brie yelled at the gray cloud. "Or she gets super gassy."

The smoke in Brie's bedroom cleared, revealing the ninja and dog. "Where is it?" the ninja asked.

"Kitchen counter," Brie said.

The ninja and the pup poofed out again. She reappeared with the pink dog in one arm and the food in the other.

She spoke slowly. "Wise ninja lesson number two: stealth is impossible when one is suffering from indigestion."

The ninja and Duchess vanished for the third and final time.

"Wait! Who are you?" Brie yelled.

There was no response.

"And aren't you going to untie me?" Brie cried at no one as the smoke dissipated entirely.

Suddenly, out of the nothingness, a tiny kunai knife sailed through the air. It sliced precisely through the rope binding Brie's arms to her sides. Brie shook her arms free of the rope. It dropped to the floor. The pointed, patterned, silver blade stuck into a box of tissues sitting on her bedside table.

Brie pulled a couple of torn tissues from the box and wrapped her hand with them before pulling out the small, sharp knife. The ninja wore black gloves, so there probably weren't any fingerprints on the kunai, but it was worth taking precautions.

The handle was wrapped tightly in black cloth. The shiny, Damascus steel blade was engraved with stripes that made Brie think of a tiger. Her father had taken the shuriken the ninja had thrown in the alley. *Who knows what he did with it? I'd better hang on to* this *clue.*

# 16

# ✳ Thorne ✳

Thorne was a master of stealth. *The fox doesn't know he has a tail.* Late Tuesday morning, his surveillance was rewarded. Demitrius Foxglove hadn't led Thorne to the "castle" where Lovey might be held. Foxglove wasn't surrounded by beautiful young women the way he was in his videos. Thorne smirked. Instead, he lived in a very normal-looking house with a dark-skinned woman who appeared too old to be his wife or girlfriend.

*But you never know . . . the guy is obsessed with Lovey.* Another possibility was that the lady could be his mob boss. *Is a Godmother a thing, like the movie* The Godfather? *Or could she be Brie's ninja?* Thorne remembered Brie saying something about the ninja being a small woman. This lady was on the tall side and roundish, in an attractively curvy way. *Foxglove fed his princess too many donuts.*

Thorne patted his belly. *This prince has had too many donuts, too.*

A van pulled up, and Foxglove trotted outside. He wore the same suit, under a wool coat that flapped open. His long legs skittered on the snow-dusted sidewalk, reminding Thorne of a grasshopper. The words Sir Lancelot's Videography Services were painted on the side of the van. The boxy vehicle was airbrushed to look like a cobblestone castle.

*Is the van the castle where Foxglove keeps his princesses?* Thorne's stomach churned at the thought of the activities that might have taken place inside the van with the fancy paint job. *These men may have committed crimes even worse than kidnapping Lovey Dearheart.*

Thorne tailed Foxglove and the driver, following them to the Citadel Mall.

Despite its reputation for being rough, it was the last thriving indoor shopping center in Colorado Springs. Until recently, soldiers stationed at the nearby Fort Carson Army Base were forbidden from hanging out there. Maybe the authorities had cracked down on questionable activities, judging by the lifting of the ban. Although Foxglove's appearance here might cast some doubt on that hypothesis.

*Seems like the kind of place a mobster might hang out.* And a van coated in nerd paint made a great cover.

After the guys unloaded film equipment from the van and were a distance away from the vehicle, Thorne peeked into its windows. The van looked empty of passengers. In fact, it didn't appear to have enough room to hold captives. No mattress. No pillows. Just built in shelves with lots of electronics, cables, and microphones.

"Lovey?" Thorne called out. *Just in case.*

No response.

He walked around the entire van, pounding its sides with his fist. "Anybody in there?" he yelled.

Silence.

There was nothing more Thorne could accomplish here without attracting attention to himself. He dashed to catch up with Foxglove inside the mall.

From the many tutorials Thorne had viewed, Foxglove spent a nauseating amount of time filming himself talking to women in public places.

Foxglove called the videographer with the castle-van

Lance. Not Sir Lancelot, even though that was the name printed on the side of his van. Lance had a video camera resting on his narrow shoulder. His red hair was tied up in a man bun, and his beard was as patchy as a teenager's. But it was long and thick where it actually grew. Round-framed glasses emphasized his perpetually surprised expression.

Lance filmed Foxglove testing out pick-up lines and asking women questions about qualities they liked in men. The ladies loved Foxglove. After exchanging socials, the women wandered off.

Foxglove turned to the camera. "I'm on the hunt for more ladies," Foxglove said as Lance continued recording. "A castle can never have too many princesses."

Thorne could only describe the grin on Foxglove's handsome face as "lascivious." At least, he was pretty sure that was a real word. If it was, it had to be the right one to describe this guy.

Foxglove pointed toward a group of cute females wearing too much makeup and not enough clothing under their open winter coats. "Women travel in flocks like peacocks, with their finest feathers on display to attract males."

*Aren't the prettiest birds the male ones?* Thorne Googled it. *I'm right. The males have the flashy plumage.* The birds were all called peafowl, and the females were called peahens. *You're splitting hairs, Thorne. The man's a genius.*

Foxglove led his cameraman toward the food court. "It is best to approach women in one of their default habitats, like the mall. Groups can be protective of their members. But most of the time, when an attractive male approaches, they become competitive, and the group can easily be divided. Women are simple creatures that way. When hunting from a flock of women, don't be picky. The finest specimens get jealous when a male flirts with lesser specimens. Use this to your advantage."

The guy sounded like this was a nature documentary for people who had never seen women before. *Just who does this guy think he is?* Thorne thought with a mingling of disgust and admiration. He took notes on his smartphone.

"Excuse me, miss." Foxglove held a small microphone near the face of the homeliest woman in the group. "Are you eighteen years of age?"

"Yes," the lady said excitedly. Thorne was sure she was at least thirty.

The woman pulled out an ID and showed it to Foxglove.

"This can't be right," Foxglove said. "Are you sure this isn't your mother's ID?"

The woman laughed. A blush erupted on her white skin.

"Do you consent to being filmed?"

"Absolutely!"

"What kind of car does your boyfriend drive?" Foxglove gave the lady his movie star smile.

She giggled awkwardly. Before she could answer the question, a prettier woman leaned toward the mic and said, "*She doesn't have a boyfriend.*"

*Amazing.* It was working out just like Foxglove had said it would. The women acted like schoolgirls and started dividing within their group. The prettiest ones were vying for Foxglove's attention. By the end of the video, Foxglove had three of the women's numbers.

Thorne trailed the love god and his cameraman out of the mall.

"That was so cool," Lance said. "You want the usual edits?"

"Yeah, and apply some beauty filters. The first lady was rough on the eyes. They *all* need to look good for my show."

*Does Lovey have to look good for your show?* Even though Thorne hadn't found definitive evidence that Foxglove had her, the pile of unopened letters and the flyer from his shop inside Lovey's cottage could not be a coincidence. Foxglove had something to do with her disappearance.

But why? It didn't seem likely that these guys were "made men." However, mobsters had mostly gone white-collar.

*Foxglove's internet empire is about as white-collar as you can get.*

Foxglove and Lance hopped into the van. Thorne got into his car and followed. If he could keep up with those guys, he just might solve this missing person case today.

He called Brie, putting his phone in speaker mode. If this car chase didn't result in finding Lovey, Brie would need help with Duchess. *Admit it, you big lunk. You miss that little doggy.*

"How is that pink puppy?" Thorne asked. "Want me to walk Duchess while you're at work?"

"She's fine. A ninja took her."

"What?" Thorne swerved his car a little. "Can you repeat that?"

"A ninja took Duchess last night," Brie replied. "I'm pretty sure it was the same ninja that was at the bodybuilding competition last month."

"What did he look like?"

"I've already told you a million times, they're a she . . . Or someone with a girly body. Black hood, black clothes, weird shoes. Ninja."

"So you just gave Duchess to a ninja last night?" Thorne was so distracted, he nearly missed seeing the van turn at the next street light. "Without a fight?"

"Well, not exactly," Brie said with a huff. "It's complicated."

"Complicated in what way?"

"She kind of broke in," Brie said. "I mean, she didn't break anything—"

"Why didn't you call me?" Thorne sped up to pass a Jeep that had pulled in between him and the van. He made his voice sound a little calmer than he felt and asked, "Are you okay?"

"Yes, Dad. She only came for the dog."

"I think she was in my house last night, too." Thorne shuddered. "Someone stole the dog bed while I was watching a ninja movie."

"Was Tommy the Tiger in it?" Brie asked.

"You mean Tommy Tigerclaw?"

"Whatever."

"How did you hear about him?" Thorne asked. The movie he watched was so low quality.

"Marty Strong has all his old-fashioned box tape thingies."

"The guy you went on your first date with? Barry's grandson?" Thorne made the connection. "Are you talking about VHS cassettes?"

"Yeah! Those," Brie said brightly. "He said they're super rare or something. By the way, have you ever heard of the No Boys Allowed Club?"

"No."

A Colorado Springs Police Department cruiser pulled alongside Thorne. *Don't make eye contact.* Thorne stared straight ahead at the castle van in front of him, cruising swiftly down Academy Boulevard.

"I'm surprised," Brie said. "They used to be all over the news. It was super mysterious because most of the women crooks were never caught. They've got to be senior citizens now. Are you sure you don't remember this, Dad? You were alive back in the seventies and eighties when they were active."

"I was a baby in the seventies!" Thorne bristled. "And just because I was alive in the eighties, doesn't mean I was watching the news."

When he wasn't at school being an average student, Thorne had been hanging out at arcades, getting good at a newly invented pastime called video games.

Thorne continued, "I'm not that old."

"Fifty is old, but that's besides the point," Brie said, "There was a mobster-type gang based out of Colorado Springs back then. Wouldn't it be weird if any of the women gangsters were living at Hummingbird Gardens today?"

Thorne thought of Demetrius Foxglove's roommate, but she seemed too young. Closer to Thorne's age. "Can you text me the name of that gang? I'm driving now, but I want to do some research later."

"Will do. But hey, my break time is over. I've gotta go. Bye!"

Brie hung up.

Two car-lengths ahead of Thorne, the van cruised through a green light. The light flashed yellow as Thorne reached the intersection. The cop car was still next to him. He had no choice but to stop. He sat, watching the van shrink in the distance and turn off the large, busy street.

*I can still catch them.* Thorne squeezed the steering wheel tightly and took a risky glance at the police car. The officer was already staring at him.

*Act normal.* Thorne smiled and waved. The officer nodded back and typed something into his dashboard computer.

The light was taking forever to change. Thorne's mind raced through his conversation with Brie. He could make sense of mobsters, but ninjas? His heart sank at the idea that Duchess had been stolen by one. *Am I really ready to accept Brie's ninja tales?* He still hadn't seen one in real life.

Last month, Thorne acquired ninja related evidence during a different case. He never got an explanation for why Barry had left celery bitten into a shuriken shape in his car. And Thorne still had the real ninja star he found in the alley. It made sense that Marty had Tommy Tigerclaw tapes thanks to the influence of Foxglove. But what did those videos have to do with a real ninja kidnapping purse puppies? *Or senior citizens?*

The long light finally turned green and Thorne got back into tracking mode. He turned off Academy Boulevard onto the side street Foxglove had taken.

The police car followed. Its lights flashed.

"Blast it all!" Thorne exclaimed as he pulled over.

A hefty fine for expired plates ended Thorne's car chase. He put the ticket in his glove compartment to deal with when he got another paying job.

# 17

# ❋ Lovey ❋

Lovey had kept her promise to Randall, but it was challenging to hold her tongue. Now that they were here, maybe he would tell his parents about his high school production himself. This was the big dress rehearsal, after all. Surely his theater group would be practicing their skit tonight.

The family took Lovey with them to the Juniper Breeze High School theater Tuesday night to practice for the Valentine's Showcase. Each performing group had been assigned a time to use the stage for dress rehearsals. Lovey had seen the schedule days ago, but had been laser focused on her class. The HMCA dance came right after the Hoffmans. Lovey felt a glimmer of hope.

*They'll see me. They'll rescue me.* Although she wasn't sure she needed rescuing. The family was so sweet, she wished she could stay. *I just need Duchess.* Two full days without her pink poodle had been agonizing.

Lovey tried not to feel empathy for her captors, but it couldn't be helped. Despite her growing affection for the Hoffmans, Lovey would leave as soon as her dance class arrived. Her only regret was not resolving things for Randall.

The sheet of paper handed out with tonight's rehearsal schedule did not list any high school performances. She frowned as she tried to recall any mention of the high school skit in which Randall claimed he was starring. Maybe she simply overlooked the other performances.

*Why would Randall make up something like this?* Their heart-to-heart had felt real. Was the teen that proficient of an actor? Lovey couldn't ask about it now, or she would break her solemn promise to Randall.

Hopefully, introducing the family to *The Phantom of the Opera* last night would set them all on the right path to accept the "alternative" boy. And if not, she had one last trick up her sleeve.

Before the family climbed the steps onto the stage, she placed a hand on Harry's arm.

"I had a successful TV show for twenty years. You need to balance the sweetness of your act with a little bit of sour. It will provide depth to your story."

"The old lady, er, Lovey is right," Randall said. "She's an expert."

"Lovey, I can't say I agree. But if we're all going to be a part of this same big wonderful family, we have to be willing to compromise," Harry said. "What do you suggest?"

"Here's what I envision." Lovey closed her eyes and spread out her hands. "The Hoffman family is in the middle of *Singin' in the Rain* when Randall steps to one side. The spotlight follows him while the rest of the family softens into shadow." Lovey opened her eyes. "Randall sings *Send in the Clowns* in a somber tone. Then he rejoins the rest of the family and completes the upbeat rain song."

"But that's so sad," Chrissy said. "And clowns are strange."

"Yeah," Randall said, "but the aesthetic . . . it's legit! I could do some sweet makeup. And my favorite band, Heaven's Hellscape, made a cover of the song. So I know all the words. It's a high-key vibe."

*What?* Lovey nodded, pretending to understand Randall's excited speech.

"Won't this make a joke of our performance?" Harry asked with a frown.

Sally's lips pulled to one side with distaste, and yet she seemed to be considering Lovey's suggestion. She tapped a finger against her chin. "Interesting." Sally looked at Harry. "The contrast Lovey wants. It's powerful."

"I don't know, darling." Harry shook his head. "It's just not what the Hoffman family is known for."

"We're not known at all." Sally added softly, "It would be nice to be noticed for once."

"I like it," Randall said. "If we use Lovey's idea, I'll work really hard on the happy parts of the skit."

Chrissy tugged on her father's sleeve. "It's okay, Daddy. Randy needs to have fun, too! He sings pretty good when he tries."

Randall didn't correct his sister's use of his nickname, for once.

"I'll probably regret this," Harry said. "But give it a go, Randy."

Lovey did a little happy dance as she stepped off stage and into the seating area. The family began the rollicking song while twirling yellow vinyl umbrellas that were so shiny, they appeared wet. Then the music switched to a peculiar rock-and-roll version of the clown song that Lovey had never heard. Randall put so much emotion into his performance that it was riveting to watch.

*But I can't linger.*

The whole family was so focused, they must have been confident she would stay put. They were wrong to trust her.

# 18

# ✳ Brie ✳

*I need to stop answering Dad's phone calls while I'm at work.* All day Tuesday, she had been preoccupied with worrying about Lovey, Duchess, gangsters, and ninjas. Every time she attempted to do research on her phone, an HMCA patron would pop up at her desk needing her attention. And her evening was already spoken for with the dress rehearsal.

*Is Dad right? Should I have fought to keep the poodle?* Brie reasoned she didn't stand a chance against the weapon-wielding ninja. *That kunai could have been stuck in me, not a tissue box.*

Trying hard to ignore her father's implied criticism, Brie packed up her tote bag at 6:00 PM. The seniors' dress rehearsal was scheduled for 7:00. The high school was very close to the HMCA. Rather than going all the way home to fix a healthy meal, Brie hit up a nearby drive-thru offering Valentine-themed drinks she had been wanting to try.

For her meal, she chose the healthiest-looking item on the menu, a tuna melt, to balance out the sugary drink she ordered. The sandwich included lettuce and tomato. *It's basically a salad smashed inside a croissant.*

The drive-thru was shockingly fast. Brie arrived at the Juniper Breeze High School theater forty-five minutes early. The HMCA van was still nowhere in sight in the dimly lit parking lot.

The campus brought back memories from when she was in high school. She had very few friends, and hadn't participated in any extracurricular activities. *I didn't even go to prom.*

She did a little math and blanched. *I graduated from high school seven years ago.* She had been an adult for what seemed like a long time. *And how much have I actually lived since then?*

Unwilling to meditate on the thought further, Brie brought up the video of the seniors' dance on her phone and tried to focus.

While she watched, she unwrapped her sandwich and took a bite. The texture of the soft, melty cheese contrasted perfectly with the flaky albacore tuna and crisp lettuce. The tomato provided a touch of sweetness. There was almost too much mayonnaise, but it moistened the dry, buttery croissant. *Delicious!*

Her mind wandered to thoughts about the missing seniors. How would a true crime podcaster analyze this mystery? What facts did Brie have? Barry was missing for a week, but he came back. *Lovey is missing now.* A ninja was involved both times. Who could this petite, athletic person be?

Poppy had been on her radar since January, and was still at the top of her list. With the new information she'd learned about the girls' mob in Colorado Springs, Brie expanded her suspect list.

*What about Diana Diamond?* She was the right size and had a tough demeanor. And she was the right age to have been a member of the No Boys Allowed Club. Was that too obvious? Brie thought someone on the lam from the law would try to disguise herself better.

Speaking of disguises, Sam Slate had an entire room full of costumes. Would a nonbinary person have been accepted as a member of the No Boys Allowed Club during that era? *Maybe.* And the cookie lady might only be pretending to be frail and anonymous. *She could be a criminal mastermind. Maybe that's why I can never remember her name.*

Then again, the ninja might not be connected to Hummingbird Gardens or the HMCA at all. *Even though both of the seniors who went missing are patrons?*

But why would a ninja with evil intentions care about reuniting an old lady with her poodle?

Dad trusted his gut feelings. So did Brie. *Unless it's the tuna talking.* Her inner detective was telling her Lovey was okay. But she still had a burning desire to know where she was. Because she doubted the dance instructor was at that romance convention.

Contemplating this mystery that was so close to home, Brie nibbled the last bite out of the sandwich wrapper. She washed it down with the large, iced, strawberry cold brew coffee she had purchased from the drive-thru. Brie only ordered it because it was a pretty, pink, temporary menu item for Valentine's Day. The drink was so sugary that the sweetness almost made up for the odd flavor. She shivered as she gave herself a brain freeze.

*Bad choice. I should have gotten a hot drink.* It was a chilly night. *I bet the school is warm.*

Brie wanted to go inside, but she didn't want to disturb the group using the theater ahead of the seniors. But what if the HMCA van parked on the other side of the building, and the seniors were already here. It was at least worth a look. Brie stepped out of her vehicle and into the cold. If the dance class wasn't there, she could always go back to her car.

The high school's front doors were unlocked. Brie heard music coming from the theater.

# 19

# ✳ Lovey ✳

Lovey heard one of the theater doors open. She saw a brown pompom of hair bounce into the auditorium. *Brie Bramble?* The poor dear girl just couldn't stay up on Lovey and Sam's attempts at a makeover.

Brie paced near the exit, glancing around like she was looking for someone. Before Lovey could call out to her, and violate the serenity of the stage, the young woman ducked back out of the theater.

Perhaps Brie was here because of the HMCA class. It was only 6:30 PM, and Lovey remembered scheduling the bus to arrive no more than ten minutes before 7:00. Maybe Lovey's students had been impatient and decided to come even earlier.

The Hoffmans were so immersed in their rehearsal that there was no way they'd notice Lovey making her escape. She had to do this quietly.

*Do I really want to do this?* Her heart was breaking. But this whole situation was wrong. She had to get back to her normal life. *To Duchess.*

Lovey got up. Hopefully, she could catch up to Brie. The high school theater exit was near the powder rooms, so if anyone saw her, hopefully they would assume she was headed there.

She passed several movie posters from obscure productions.

First was *A Die Hard Musical Parody* with a man wearing a blood splattered undershirt and suspenders, singing into a gun. Next came *Bloody, Bloody Andrew Jackson*, which was apparently a musical comedy chronicling the life of the American president responsible for the Trail of Tears. The last poster stopped her in her tracks.

*A ninja?* He reminded Lovey of a breakdancer with a neon yellow fishnet crop top and a bright green headband. But he wore the same kind of black pants the ninja who kidnapped Lovey wore. On his feet were those weird ninja shoes, with the slit in the middle that made them look like a person had two large toes instead of five small ones on each foot. But no hood hid his face. He was a brown man with rippling abdominals and a million-dollar smile. He held a ninja star in his hand. The poster said, *Tommy Tigerclaw: He Who Follows the Shogun.*

Lovey's mind whirred for a moment, but she pulled her focus back to catching up with Brie. She took one last peek at the Hoffmans as she reached for the exit door handle. She pushed it open and—

"Yip!"

"Duchess!" Lovey cried as she reached down, then folded the pup into her arms. Duchess wasn't wearing the faux fur coat and matching boots Lovey had dressed her in the morning of the kidnapping. Instead, she had on a sparkly red sweater. Hopefully, that meant she'd been well cared for. *Not that well.* Duchess's accessories had been neglected. The red rosette that matched the sweater was missing.

The ninja stood nearby, her black-gloved hands folded across her womanly chest.

Lovey frowned. "You!"

"You weren't trying to escape now, were you?" the ninja asked in her strange voice.

"I, I—" Lovey's words were cut off by the sound of Chrissy's applause. The Hoffmans must have finished practicing their routine. "I just needed some fresh air."

Lovey peeked around the ninja. Brie was gone.

The ninja handed Lovey a bag of Delicate Tummy Gourmet Crumbles dog kibble. "You need to stay within sight of your new family."

*My new family.* Lovey tried to disconnect with the idea, but it resonated within her. And with sweet little Duchess licking her cheek, Lovey was losing her resolve to leave. But why was this so-called ninja calling the shots? Lovey glanced back at one of the movie posters.

"Are you an actor?" Lovey pointed to Tommy Tigerclaw. "Like him?"

"No. And that wasn't just a movie," the ninja said. "Tommy Tigerclaw is real."

Lovey heard the tapping of shoes on the hallway floor.

"Grandma! There you are! Our turn on the stage is done." Chrissy's voice called from behind her. "We're gonna go get petit fours at La Baguette!"

Lovey's desire to leave had melted away with the warmth of Duchess in her arms. And she adored the local French restaurant.

"I have a surprise!" Lovey held out Duchess. Her puppy smiled at the child and wagged her tail.

"Adorbs!" Chrissy exclaimed. She put her face up to Duchess, and the pup licked her cheeks in a frenzy. Chrissy laughed. "Where did she come from?"

"The ninja returned Duchess to me," Lovey said.

"Where is the ninja?" Chrissy asked, looking around the hallway.

Lovey turned back around to thank the ninja, but it was as if she had never been there.

# 20

# ❋ Brie ❋

A gust of icy wind pounded against Brie's Subaru. She had retreated back to her car out of respect for the Hoffmans' stage time. Brie had her heater on blast so she wasn't that cold anymore. However, she wished she had used the bathroom while she was inside the school. *Maybe I shouldn't have ordered a large drink.*

Headlights swept across the asphalt. The HMCA van finally pulled into the almost empty parking lot.

The door opened. Brie hopped out of her car and hurried across the pavement.

"Hi Brie!" Ramona stepped out of the driver's seat. "Can you assist some of our superstars out of the van?"

Brie helped the dance students who needed a hand down the steps. She offered a supporting arm, unfolded walkers, and handed seniors canes. Then she and Ramona led the group indoors. The Hoffmans must have finished during the slow debarkation of the Hummingbird crowd. The stage was empty and ready for the dancers.

"Can we please get started?" Diana Diamond asked impatiently.

Brie studied the stern black woman. Mobster? Ninja? Or just a senior citizen who valued efficiency? Sam and the cookie lady looked as innocent as they always did. The seniors seemed like the dance was really important to them. Making Lovey disappear was working directly against that goal. Unless this was all an act.

Diana continued, "This is one of our few chances to practice on the real stage. We only have one hour before the kids from the Barbara Ellis Studio get here."

"Line up," Sam Slate said in their bland-sounding voice. "Get in position. Don't forget your accessories!"

"Here are feather boas," Layton said as he handed out the colorful props. "And grab a fan."

The seniors lined up and grabbed ostrich plume fans and draped feather boas around their necks. While the seniors prepared to rehearse, Brie wandered around the theater. She was desperate to find a restroom. As she entered a hallway, a flash of color on the floor caught her eye. Some dancer had lost a costume accessory. It looked oddly familiar. Brie picked up the flower.

*Red ribbon. Silver sparkles. Duchess's rosette! No way.*

Brie brought it into the light to have a better look. A curl of pink dog hair was stuck to the underside of the flower decoration. If Duchess was here, did that mean Lovey was here, too?

"Brie!" A voice echoed through the nearly empty theater. "We're ready."

"Where are you?" another senior called. "Hurry up!"

Brie pocketed the red rosette, and grimaced. She should have focused on finding - and using - the facilities. *I can hold it a little longer.* She tightened her resolve muscles and moved toward a seat in the audience next to Ramona.

Before she could sit, Diana called out, "Get up here, Brie!"

"But I'm not in the Showcase," she protested.

"We need you to lead us through the routine," Layton said. "We've never performed this on an actual stage."

Ramona gave Brie a gentle push. "You'd better get up

there!"

Brie waited for everyone to take their places while Layton brought up the song on his smartphone. He got into position, then held his finger over the screen.

"Ready, everyone?"

A chorus of "yes," "yeah," and "sure" rolled over the stage. Layton punched the play button. "You Sexy Thing," by Hot Chocolate, blared through the speaker. Brie tried to shake her booty in rhythm with the music, but she kept falling off the beat. *Why am I so bad at this?* It wasn't like she didn't have enough of a butt to shake. Brie had been endowed with a round rump of more than adequate proportions required for the dance.

*Concentrate!*

The music shut off abruptly. Layton waved his phone, then folded his arms across his large tummy.

"I can't follow the routine if you keep changing the choreography," he complained.

Brie wasn't changing anything. She was just that bad.

"I'm trying my best—"

"Good evening!" Officer Riggs Saito waved his hand at the class. "Sorry I'm late. I just got off work, and I had to change out of my uniform before coming over."

*Yikes! How long has he been watching?* Brie was mortified that the smooth-dancing Riggs had seen her fumbling attempts again. *He looks so good in workout clothes.* Brie blinked a few times and shook her head, forcing herself to look away. The last thing she needed was to zone out on stage in front of everyone.

"We're just getting started," Layton said.

"We've already wasted ten minutes." Diana tapped her smartwatch.

Sam fluttered their fingers at Riggs. "Can you demonstrate those dance moves you showed us?"

"My grandson is not your puppet," George Saito said with a frown. "He's a cop." George looked up at Riggs. "I've had enough of this nonsense. Take me home."

"You can sit with me and watch if you don't want to dance," Ramona said from her seat in the audience. "And we would love it if you rode the bus with us back to Hummingbird Gardens when we're finished."

"No," George said. "I don't want to dance, and I don't want to watch these foolish old people cavort about on stage. I want to go home to my house, not that lousy apartment my ungrateful grandson condemned me to."

Riggs looked like he had been slapped, his face scrunched as though he was in physical pain. "You need a walker now, Grandpa. There's no way to navigate your house with all those stairs. Hummingbird Gardens is your home."

"Against my will."

It was a story Brie had heard too often. Seniors who couldn't manage living in their houses unassisted anymore resented being talked into moving into senior apartments. Most quickly realized Hummingbird Gardens was a wonderful place. Some elderly people were just old cranks, not happy wherever they lived. Brie suspected George might be one of the perpetually disgruntled types.

The cookie lady placed a gentle hand on George's arm. "You signed up for the class. We can't do the show without you now. We need you."

"We're a fun group," Layton said. "Give us a chance, George."

"It's not like I have a choice," George grumbled. "But mark my words, one of you is going to throw a hip out of socket."

"Exercise will keep you limber," Layton said. The large man dropped down into the splits. Everyone gasped and then clapped when he stood up again. "Dance is excellent for maintaining the muscles needed for stability."

"That's what this is for." George gripped his walker.

"Dancing burns calories." The cookie lady held a plate of red and pink sprinkle-coated treats in front of George. "So we can eat more cookies."

*Where did she get those from?* Brie didn't remember her walking in with the platter.

George scowled at her, but snatched a heart-shaped cookie from the plate. He took a savage bite. Pink sprinkles scattered like shrapnel. Brie thought a smile might be tugging at his lips, but he quickly suppressed it.

"When is Lovey going to return?" Riggs asked. When Brie didn't answer, he scanned the faces of the class. "Has anyone heard from her yet?"

"There's nothing to worry about," Ramona said. "Lovey must be having such a wonderful time at the Ripped Bodice Romance convention, she hasn't had a spare moment to call us."

"I talked to the convention director," Riggs said. "Lovey isn't registered. Maybe it's time to file a missing person's report."

"That's not a bad idea, Officer Saito. But I don't believe that's necessary," Ramona said. "Lovey is a private person. She probably doesn't use her real name at high-profile events."

The cookie lady nodded. "Celebrities are often very guarded about their personal lives. But I don't understand why she didn't let us know her plans."

The other seniors shook their heads sadly.

Brie couldn't hold back. The seniors' stress levels were escalating. She had to share her information, as little as it was.

"I, uh, heard she's fine," Brie said.

"You know something!" Layton pointed at Brie. "Spill it!"

The class surrounded Brie, clamoring for news. She held up her hands. "I can't give you any details."

"That's not acceptable," George said. "You're withholding facts needed by the police to solve this case."

"Well, technically," Riggs began, "there is no case without an official report."

"Thorne Bramble is on the job," the cookie lady said. "He accepted a retainer of peanut brittle to investigate."

George snorted.

Riggs took Brie's arm and pulled her away from the rest of the group. Brie's heart pounded. *He's touching me! And looking at me!* Riggs's black hair shone, reflecting the stage light. His almond-shaped eyes bored into her soul. *Yes. You can have all of my secrets. You can have—*

He bent down near her ear. *He's so close!* Brie dared not breathe. She hadn't brushed her teeth after the tuna melt she had for dinner. The strawberry iced coffee probably combined with it to create toxic breath fumes.

"We need to talk," Riggs whispered to Brie. He tugged her behind the heavy black stage curtain.

Which might have been a prelude to a romantic interlude, if George hadn't followed with his robin's egg blue rollator, the wheels squeaking across the wooden stage. Brie really wished the cranky old man wasn't there to listen and offer his insulting opinions.

"What did you hear about Lovey?" Riggs asked in a low voice.

"That she's fine." Brie repeated her earlier words.

Riggs didn't look convinced. "Who told you that?"

"Someone I trust."

"So you aren't going to give me any details." Riggs looked frustrated.

"I don't really have any. I just have a gut feeling," Brie said, echoing her father. *That's not the only thing going on with my gut.* More like her bladder. Her temporary reprieve from her bathroom needs was over. She started wiggling in a potty dance.

"That sounds stupid," George muttered. "But what do you expect from a stoner?" He bobbed his head up and down, staring at Brie, who was now bouncing from one foot to the other with her legs crossed. "Maybe it's worse than I thought. Amphetamines?"

"That's enough, Grandpa. Please, Brie, explain."

*Hold it!* Brie commanded herself. Tensing every muscle she had on the lower half of her body, she pulled the dog collar adornment from the pocket of her HMCA hoodie. "This belongs to Duchess."

"The Duchess of York?" George asked. "Sarah Ferguson, AKA Fergie? What does she have to do with Lovey Dearheart? Fergie isn't even a duchess anymore."

Brie's head spun for a moment, trying to make the leaps in logic with the retired detective.

"Uh, no. See that strand of curly pink fur on the back of the decoration? That's the same color as Lovey's poodle, Duchess. I found it here, in the hallway."

Riggs lifted the accessory from Brie's palm, holding it close to his eyes. "All this proves is that something pink was here in this theater," Riggs said. "It doesn't tell us what this strand came from."

"It certainly doesn't pinpoint Lovey's poodle." George gripped his walker and leaned forward. "Have you seen all the kids with pink hair nowadays? There are plenty of ways to test whether this is human or dog hair, or even a fabric fiber. But it's probably a waste of the police department's time."

Brie felt herself begin to doubt the collar decoration was the dog's, even though she had clipped it onto Duchess's collar last night with her own hands. There was more to her story. *The ninja.* However, George was so difficult to talk to. If she could just get Riggs alone . . .

"When did you find this?" Riggs asked.

Brie said, "Maybe ten minutes ago."

"And you didn't pursue the clue further?" George asked.

"The class yelled for me," Brie said. "I didn't have the chance to look around."

"You can look now," George said.

"But they want me on stage," Brie said.

"My grandson will lead the rehearsal." George turned his rollator around. "Lovey isn't here, and that's not a clue."

*It's a good thing Detective Saito retired. He's got serious confirmation bias.* Brie had learned from true crime podcasts that investigators sometimes let their preconceived theories blind them to real suspects and clues.

"I'll handle the class," Riggs said. "Brie, can you return to where you found the flower thing? If you see anything, let me know." Riggs turned back to face the dancers and clapped his hands. "Hey, everyone. We'll get to the bottom of this. Right now, how about we finish up this rehearsal?"

Layton hit play, and Riggs started gyrating and shaking his hips.

The moment to tell Riggs about the ninja was gone. Brie skulked to the high school bathroom and released a torrent of artificially strawberry-colored fluid from her tortured bladder. She didn't want to teach Lovey's class, but she found herself annoyed by being pushed aside. Especially because she made a special trip out here this evening after work. She wasn't being paid for this. *Neither is Riggs.* However, the seniors loved him. They were showering him with their admiration. They merely tolerated Brie.

After leaving the bathroom, she began hunting for more clues. She scanned hallways, the dressing rooms, the lighting and props areas. She scoured every inch of the high school theater.

But there was no sign of Lovey.

# 21

# ✳ Lovey ✳

At the dress rehearsal last night, Lovey had lost her resolve to escape. Wednesday, her heart was brimming with happiness. Her one great fear had been for Duchess's well-being. Now that the puppy sat at her feet, Lovey's anxiety completely dissolved. The ninja had even assured Lovey that her dance class was being guided by an expert.

The Hoffman family had accepted Lovey's poodle into their home last night without question. Chrissy was delighted with the puppy's many stylish clothing options, including the cute little snow boots.

The only problem so far was the family over-pampering Duchess. Lovey had to be stern about not allowing the family to feed her unapproved snacks. The poodle suffered severe digestive issues when fed people food.

"Can I give Duchess a doggy biscuit?" Chrissy asked.

"She's had enough treats," Lovey told the child. "Any more, and her little tummy will burst."

"Let's start a movie while we're waiting for the lasagna to finish baking," Harry said. "Chrissy gets to choose the movie tonight."

"I wanna see *Dog Man: The Musical*." Chrissy jumped up and down.

"It's family-friendly," Sally told Lovey. "Not scary, like that musical you asked us to watch. Even though I loved it."

"Ugh. A happy musical," Randall said. "But if there's a dog in it, I guess it's okay."

The kids settled on the sofa next to Lovey with Duchess tucked between them.

While Harry scrolled through their streaming service for the movie, the kids asked Lovey questions about the poodle.

"How did her fur get so pink?" Randall asked. "It doesn't grow like that, right?"

"Duchess has naturally white fur," Lovey said. "It readily takes any color dye."

"She looks good in pink," Sally said.

"I'd like to see her in black," Randall said with a grin.

"No!" Chrissy wailed. "I like pink!"

Duchess had an entire wardrobe in Lovey's cottage. The ninja had only brought a few outfits and Duchess's dog bed to the Hoffmans' home. Lovey wondered what had happened to the brand-new red rosette with silver sparkles that matched the sweater Duchess was wearing now. The absence of the decoration indicated a serious neglect of wardrobe harmony. *Sam would definitely not approve.* Lovey smiled.

"We can compromise. When in doubt, accessorize. Harry, please give us a moment." Lovey led the kids to her room. Duchess followed, her pink toenails clicking on the parquet floor. "My clothing choices aren't all pink, Randall. Black goes very well with Duchess's shade. Let's see what we can find."

Lovey was concerned at first about letting the children loose in her closet and drawers. However, they were musical theater kids, so they had an inherent respect for costuming, despite their eager fingers touching everything.

"How about this?" Randall held up one of Lovey's sequined blouses. "It's black."

"That's too big for Duchess," Chrissy said. "I like this."

The girl had selected a pink silk scarf with narrow threads

of black.

"Too much pink," Randall said.

"You can see, though," Lovey said, "how pink and black make a nice combination."

"Then how about this?" Randall found a shiny black satin bow attached to a hair clip.

"Ugh!" Chrissy cried.

"Give it a chance," Lovey said. She clipped the bow to Duchess's collar. "With a bit of adjustment, this will work."

While she played with the bow, making it into a safe and secure addition to the poodle's collar, Lovey felt a contentment she had rarely known.

The opportunity to have her own children and grandchildren may have passed her by, but the ninja thought Lovey and the Hoffman family were a perfect match. Their affection for only the most syrupy of musicals was problematic for their son, Randall. What was Lovey's contribution to this household? How did she fit in? The retired chef Layton often said the most delicious meals needed a balance of sweet and spicy.

"Mom," Randall said. "Dad. Look! Duchess is really cute now."

"Isn't she!" Chrissy gushed. "Black and pink go great together."

*Like sweet and spicy.* Lovey felt Chrissy's instant acceptance and love like a warm, melty, chocolate chip cookie. Randall was more like a jalapeno popper. *Approach with caution.*

Randall was the spice in this family. His own parents didn't seem to understand what he brought to the Hoffman recipe.

The family needed her, maybe even more than she needed them. Lovey was ready.

"Before you start the movie," she said, "where is that ninja contract?"

# 22

# ✳ Brie ✳

After the Wednesday dance rehearsal in the HMCA classroom, Brie felt drained. Riggs had been on duty, so he didn't steal the show this time. All eyes were on Brie's failures. George was more than happy to point out every missed step. *Why doesn't he just teach the class since he clearly has a better grasp of things. Even with his hands grasping the handles of his rollator.*

Brie desperately wanted Lovey to come back and free her from the purgatory of teaching cranky senior citizens how to gyrate.

*Only three more days. After the Valentine's Showcase, I'll be free.*

Brie pinned up a flyer for the spring break basketball camp on a bulletin board by the glass doors into the swimming pool. A swim might be good stress relief. Maybe she'd stick around after work and splash a few laps. Or just float. Brie looked longingly at the pool. Her curly hair didn't love chlorine, but what did that matter? She couldn't do a thing with it anyway.

A couple of kids jumped into the pool and raced down one of the lap lanes. Brie could see their muscles bunching up with every stroke. Kids that chiseled could only mean one thing. *Those are Barry Strong's grandkids. Barry's here.*

The elderly bodybuilder went missing like Lovey last

month, returning a week later reunited with long-lost family no one had ever heard him mention. Maybe Barry knew something about Lovey's disappearance.

Brie opened the glass doors and stepped into the reassuring chemical fumes that told HMCA patrons the pool was clean. She walked directly to Barry, unfazed by his microscopic Speedo. The man was seventy, but he was built like a Greek god. *If any Greek gods were as bald as cueballs.*

"Grandpa, who won?" a little boy sputtered. He dangled from the edge of the pool, out of breath.

"Scarlett," Barry said.

"Yay!" the little girl, Scarlett, exclaimed.

"But it was a close one, Scott!" Barry reached down and gave the boy a high five.

"Let's race again!" Scott said.

"On your mark, get set, go!" Barry said.

The siblings went splashing down the lap lane.

Brie spoke to Barry. "Having fun?"

"These are some wonderful kids." Barry beamed.

Brie knew they weren't Barry's only grandkids. His relationship with his adult grandson was problematic.

"How's Marty?" Brie asked. The guy might have told the police that he wanted a restraining order against Brie, but she still wondered about him. *Morbid curiosity?* He did invite her on her first date after all. There must have been a crumb of affection on his part. *Until things went drastically wrong.*

"Marty's got a long way to go, but I've got confidence he'll get there," Barry said. "Learning the Colorado Springs bus transit system, and attending his Gamblers' Anonymous meetings, take up a lot of his time."

"That's good," Brie said. "Do you know what happened to his tiger car?"

Brie had watched the orange and black stripey car get towed away when it had been repoed.

"I haven't heard anything. Marty isn't talking to me much

these days." Barry looked wistful.

"Don't worry, Barry," Brie said. "He'll come around. He's not as much of a tough guy as he pretends to be."

To Brie, Marty seemed like a vulnerable little boy playing at being a big bad man.

"You're so right." Barry nodded. "Maybe facing some real-life challenges will help him finally finish growing up. He's always been the entrepreneurial type. He could start his own business or something. You know, I met a guy who raises ostriches for a living?"

"Ostriches?" Brie crinkled her nose. "Is he a zookeeper?"

"Nope. I guess people like the meat and eggs. Those giant eggs must make some serious omelets. He also hauls truckloads of the feathers around. I guess there's a demand for them in Denver."

"Come to think of it, we use them here in the Springs, too. The senior jazz class is full of ostrich plume fans. I bet they came from your friend. How many ostrich farms can there possibly be in Colorado?"

"A lot more than you'd think."

*Weird.* This was interesting, but it wasn't helping Brie with her investigation.

"Barry, may I ask you something?"

"You need some bodybuilding advice? Like your father?" The corners of Barry's blue-gray eyes crinkled as he smiled.

"Not exactly," Brie said. "This is more personal."

"What is it, then? I'd love to help."

"How did you get reunited with your family?"

"It was easy. I just needed some help making a connection of the heart."

*Vague.* Brie tried being direct.

"Did a ninja help you make that connection?"

Barry laughed, but he didn't say no. He looked away, watching the children splashing in the pool.

"Please, Barry. I need your help. Lovey is missing."

"I heard," Barry said. He turned, locking his eyes onto Brie's. "You don't need my help, and neither does Lovey. If there's a ninja involved in her disappearance, you have nothing to worry about." He winked.

"Grandpa! Get in! We want to race *you* now!" Scarlett yelled.

"Duty calls," Barry told Brie. He waved and dove into the water.

# 23

## * Thorne *

The missing senior case had nearly stalled out. Four days. *Unacceptable*. Thorne almost felt guilty for accepting the peanut brittle retainer. But he was certain the case was about to bust wide open.

Thorne slouched on the seat of his anonymous Ford Fusion Thursday in a parking space directly across from the storefront of Demetrius Foxglove's Love Parlor and Sir Lancelot's Videography Services. If he followed Foxglove's advice, he'd trade Chandos in for a chick magnet like Marty Strong's flashy orange and black Gourami FSX. But a PI needed to blend in, not stand out in a crowd. *Plus, I'd probably end up in the same situation as Marty — with a repossessed car and no wheels except for the city bus.*

Old Colorado City wasn't bustling with tourists this time of year. A guy sitting in his car eating a large order from a drive-through fried chicken finger place didn't attract attention. Down to his last finger, scraping dregs of sauce from a tiny plastic cup, he grew impatient. His butt ached.

He was concerned there might be a nefarious connection between Brie's so-called ninja and this Foxglove character. His daughter had come in contact with both, indirectly. She'd gone on a date with Marty, one of Foxglove's pathetic incel students.

*Barry's grandson, who has the complete collection of Tommy Tigerclaw ninja videos.* She claimed to have seen a ninja last month, and again Tuesday, both times while trying to locate seniors missing from Hummingbird Gardens.

What was Foxglove doing with seniors? *Does the man have some weird fetish for old people?* Thorne needed answers.

A delivery van pulled into a space close to Foxglove's Love Parlor, blocking Thorne's view of the front door.

Foxglove's business was near closing time, according to the hours stenciled on the Love Parlor's front door. The last time he had a clear view, Thorne knew Foxglove was still in the building. But with the delivery van blotting out what he needed to see, Thorne might miss the guy leaving to go on another seductive mall crawl.

Time was wasting. Out of chicken, Thorne broke off a piece of peanut brittle to fortify himself. He had to take action. Easing out of Chandos, his foot broke through the crust of ice on a puddle.

"Gadzooks!" Thorne shook his soaked shoe, bumping backward into his car. The door slammed shut. *There goes any attempt at stealth.* But no one paid any attention to him. *Slick. Still got it.*

Congratulating himself for sticking to a past New Year's Resolution to clean up his potty mouth, Thorne stepped carefully down the slushy sidewalk. As he peeked around the delivery van, Thorne's shoulders slumped. The neon sign featuring the boy and girl fox and heart logo was no longer illuminated. The paper "Open" sign by the door had been flipped to "Closed." Foxglove had given him the slip. *Again.*

Even if he'd missed Foxglove leaving, Thorne could take advantage of the man's absence to check out his business. He patted his trench coat pocket, ensuring he had his trusty new lock-picking set. Not that he had ever successfully picked a lock, but there was always a first time. He had decided it was time to graduate from paperclips, which never seemed to work for him, and invested in the small kit.

Thorne pulled out his lockpicking set and went to work. First, he inserted a hook. When that did nothing, he tried his half-diamond pick. *Speaking of Diamond. Diana could pick this lock in 2.5 seconds flat.* Where did the Hummingbird Gardens resident learn a skill like that? His thoughts flitted to Brie's information about the No Boys Allowed Club.

The sound of slushy movement approaching distracted Thorne. A grown man, clutching a briefcase, wearing office attire and a DUI ankle bracelet peddled down the sidewalk on a child's bike. He nearly side-swiped Thorne. Frozen brown muck sprayed his trench coat.

"Oh, come on!" Thorne wailed.

"Sorry, man!" The guy called out. But he didn't stop.

Thorne crouched down and went back to work on the lock. After another fruitless attempt, he pulled out his phone to watch yet another tutorial. But his screen was so badly cracked, he couldn't make out the details.

Suddenly, the door opened outward, nearly hitting him in the face, causing him to drop his phone again. It barely missed the dirty puddle beneath Thorne's soaked dress shoes. Instead, it crash-landed, bouncing twice before coming to a rest on a dry patch of hard sidewalk.

"Fiddlesticks!" Thorne bent down cautiously, prepared for sparks to erupt. He picked up the remains of his tormented phone. The screen still glowed with a glimmer of life.

A middle-aged black woman stood before Thorne in the open doorway.

*No lockpicking today.* It was both a bummer and a relief.

Thorne held his breath. *Foxglove's roommate. The Godmother?*

The woman greeted him. "I was just about to lock up, but I can handle one more customer."

*The door wasn't even locked?* Thorne hadn't thought to check because the "Open" sign flipped to "Closed."

"Welcome to Demitrius Foxglove's Love Parlor!"

Thorne stepped inside, wiping the slush off his feet on a doormat covered with hearts pierced by arrows. Nothing could help his soaked shoes and filthy trench coat.

The woman had on too much makeup, thick fake eyelashes, manicured nails that looked too long to type with, and a poofy hairstyle evoking more of the '80s than modern fashion. Thorne guessed her to be a little older than his age of fifty.

"Do you want to learn about romance, or are you here for Sir Lancelot's Videography Services?"

"Actually, I'm looking for a missing person." He flashed his PI business card. "I need to talk to Mr. Foxglove. Now."

The woman's dimpled smile vanished. "This is a legitimate facility, Mr. Bramble. You won't find any wrongdoing here. Mr. Foxglove is a very good boy, er, man."

*Awfully defensive. A sure sign that rules are being broken.*

Thorne gently tapped on his phone screen, bringing up a photo of Lovey. "Ms. Dearheart hasn't shown up to work for several days. Have you seen her?"

"What exactly are you trying to show me?" The woman squinted at Thorne's phone.

The screen had gone from spiderwebbed to pixie dust. The sputtering image on the shattered screen was so distorted it didn't resemble a human being. Thorne stashed his phone in his trench coat pocket and tried another approach.

"Lovey Dearheart, star of *The Hopeless Romantic*."

"Lovey!"

"You know her?"

"Of course," the receptionist said. "I never missed an episode of *The Hopeless Romantic* back in the nineties. Lovey Dearheart is an icon."

"But have you seen her lately?" Thorne waved a hand around. "Like here?"

"I wish! Mr. Foxglove is also a huge fan of Ms. Dearheart. He would love to meet her in person."

The woman seemed genuinely excited. *Or she's a great actress.*

"It's very important that I talk to him concerning the whereabouts of Ms. Dearheart. She's missing, and people are worried about her."

The receptionist seemed to struggle with indecision for a moment, a frown threatening to crack the spackle coating her face.

"Mr. Foxglove has been attempting to meet Lovey for some time now." She added softly, almost more to herself, "She's missing. So that's why she hasn't answered his calls or letters. That makes sense. She's not avoiding him after all." She focused on Thorne. "Mr. Foxglove also has an interest in finding Ms. Dearheart."

"If he really needs to find Lovey," Thorne said, "maybe we can help each other. I need to speak to him."

The woman brightened. "Mr. Foxglove usually spends Thursday evenings at the Pokey Cowboy downtown."

"Thank you, ma'am," Thorne said. He made his way toward the exit.

"Before you go, would you like a donut?"

"For free?"

"Of course!"

Thorne took a Boston cream from the box she held out to him.

"Be careful, it's cold and icy outside," she said as Thorne left.

Without an ounce of guilt, he took a bite. Free food didn't count on a diet. *What a sweet lady.* Thorne's gut told him nothing was amiss about her. But his PI brain made him cautious. *Don't let your guard down with this one.*

He tried not to run as he left the shop. It was only a few blocks' drive from Old Colorado City to the heart of Colorado Springs. Parking downtown could be a bear on the evenings and weekends, but this early on a Thursday might not be bad. He circled the block the cowboy bar occupied three times before giving up. He found a nearby pay parking lot.

*I wonder if the parking attendant will accept peanut brittle instead of cash?*

The kid was a stickler for the rules. Thorne reluctantly paid real money and hoped there was no cover charge at the bar.

A sandwich board on the sidewalk announced it was Ladies' Night. *Of course Foxglove is here.* Thorne was pleased to see he had just made it before having to pay to enter.

A burly bouncer was checking drivers' licenses before people went past the entrance to make sure they were old enough to drink. He waved Thorne on without asking for any identification.

"Aren't you going to check my ID?" Thorne asked.

The bouncer chuckled. "You're good to go, Grandpa."

*I guess I asked for that.* Mortified, Thorne skulked inside.

Recorded Country Western music blared from speakers while the live band set up on the small stage.

Thorne did reconnaissance. The interior was a maze of alcoves and open areas, a sea of tall round tables and stools with saddles instead of seats. There were three areas set up as bars, with shelves of liquor gleaming under strings of lights. Only one was selling drinks at this early hour.

Two years ago, the sight of the colorful bottles in dozens of shapes and sizes would have sent Thorne's cravings into overdrive. Now he only saw prettily packaged poisons and reminders of shame and loss.

One fragment of his past could still be won back. The most important part. He might be only getting paid with peanut brittle - the best peanut brittle in the universe - but finding Lovey would be another step in the process to heal his relationship with his daughter.

Thorne muttered to himself, "Where are you, Foxglove?"

Then he saw an arrow pointing to a set of stairs. Thorne looked up. The stairs led to a balcony billiard room. Thorne climbed to the top and surveyed the area below. He shook his head. The light crowd consisted of a handful of young men sporting new recruit buzzcuts. A couple women were obvious soldiers, too, with slicked back buns. Something in a soldier's posture and bearing yelled "military."

Foxglove wasn't among them. His tight dark curls were buzzed short, but not recruit style. That guy was all about fashion. He would stand out in any crowd. And he wasn't here. The receptionist, or mafia boss woman, had lied to him.

Thorne turned from the balcony railing on the upper level of the bar, prepared to take another tour of the downstairs, when a splash of color caught his eye. He pressed his hands to the railing as he spotted Foxglove down below. No one could miss him. A flashy purple-fringed Western shirt unbuttoned to his trim waist revealed abs air-brushed onto his dark skin. A shiny red cowboy hat perched on his short black curls. The skinny guy had to be wearing shoulder pads.

"Sir Lancelot" followed Foxglove. Besides being the only person with a full-sized video camera, the videographer didn't attempt a Western look. The dude stood out in a white T-shirt advertising his services. Lance's red man-bun and round glasses, magnifying his already large eyes, caught a lot of startled looks from other bar patrons.

Foxglove perched on a saddle-topped stool at a high-top table. Thorne knew from watching his tutorials that he was playing the flower, waiting for the feminine bees to be attracted to his sweet nectar. Thorne began walking downstairs, his knees complaining with every step. Before he reached the bottom, a few cowgirls had already fallen into Foxglove's trap. They stood around him, giggling.

In a scene reminding Thorne of the mall, he had to wonder whether they'd been drawn to Foxglove, or to the opportunity to preen in front of Lance's camera.

He waited for a chance to talk to Foxglove alone, but the girls kept circling him. *Like delicate butterflies about to be captured in a Venus flytrap's carnivorous jaw.* Thorne grew impatient. He was almost ready to barge in and demand a private moment with the love master when Foxglove gracefully slid off his saddle stool, like he rode horses every day.

"A moment, ladies. This cowboy needs to answer the call of nature."

He strolled toward the hallway with doors marked for Stallions and Fillies. Thorne followed. Foxglove tapped a fist against the Stallions sign with a smirk.

"That's me," he mumbled to himself.

Thorne followed the guy inside the dim bathroom. The stalls were done up with swinging saloon-style doors like he'd seen in Old West movies. He was momentarily distracted by the framed photos of scantily clad cowgirls in seductive poses.

Before Foxglove could take care of his bodily business, Thorne interrupted him. "Hey. Foxglove. We need to chat."

The man turned, his brown eyes wide with surprise under the shadow of the red cowboy hat.

"What do you want?"

"I just came from your Love Parlor," Thorne said. "You need to answer my questions."

Foxglove relaxed into a smile. "Of course. You can find answers to all your questions on my social media sites. Subscribe today for a twenty percent discount."

He pulled a coupon with a QR code from his too-tight blue jeans pocket.

"I need information of a more personal nature," Thorne said, carefully tucking the coupon into his trench coat pocket. "Don't deny it. You're attracted to senior citizens."

"What?" Foxglove's lips curled in disgust. "Even if I were, you are of the wrong, er, persuasion. No offense, sir, but I'm a heterosexual cisgendered male."

Thorne only had a vague notion of what all that meant. *He's accusing me of hitting on him . . . I think . . .*

The door to the Stallions' bathroom swung open. Thorne

sensed someone coming from behind. His gut was never wrong. He turned to see Lance aiming the video camera in his direction.

"Whoa," Thorne said. "Cameras aren't allowed in public bathrooms!"

The camera guy just stood there with his camera aimed at Thorne.

"Stalker fan!" Foxglove yelled. "Stop him!"

Foxglove weaseled his way past Thorne, out of the bathroom, and dashed onto the dance floor.

The videographer stepped aside and mumbled, "I'm just the cameraman."

Thorne ignored him and chased Foxglove. Lance didn't try to stop him.

Thorne heard the clomping of dozens of boots and spun to see Foxglove in the midst of a complicated line dance. *No problemo. I'll dance my way to the perp.*

Thorne tacked himself to the end of a line, three rows away from Foxglove, and started stamping his feet and swinging his arms. *This is easy!* Thorne thought too soon. Everyone spun around at the same time, and the line moved in the opposite direction Thorne was expecting. He was left standing by himself. He quickly ducked into the line two rows from Foxglove and started dancing again.

Foxglove was a master line dancer. But Thorne was getting the hang of it. He had just about figured it out when the DJ changed the song. The crowd stomped their boots faster than before. Someone's heel slammed onto Thorne's dress shoe.

"Frick!" Thorne cried.

No one seemed to notice the PG expletive Thorne cried out over the loud music and everyone else's happy hooting and hollering. They just kept dancing. Thorne gave up on trying to meld with their movements and moved a row closer to Foxglove. And finally, into Foxglove's row. Thorne stomped and spun around the other dancers until he was right behind him. When Foxglove turned around and saw Thorne, he jumped four feet in the air and landed off the dance floor. Foxglove ran. Thorne struggled to keep up.

He was just in time to see Foxglove attempt to blend into a crowd gathered in front of an Old West-looking bar. The man swung onto the saddle of a barstool with the grace of a gymnast sticking onto a pommel horse.

Thorne broke through the crowd and yelled, "I just have a few questions!"

Foxglove slithered off the saddle-stool and started running again. Thorne chased him, confused when the guy dipped low.

"Ow!" A dart struck Thorne in his bicep. He jerked it out and handed it back to the husky cowgirl who had just thrown it.

"That one doesn't count," she said to her companions. "That guy got in the way. I get a do-over!"

Thorne clasped a hand onto his arm where a trickle of blood dripped through his trench coat sleeve. *Wounded in the line of duty. A small price to pay to solve a case.* Were his tetanus shots up to date? He'd check on that later.

Foxglove cackled as he ran for a door beneath a red exit sign.

Thorne followed. Foxglove ran up the sidewalk, dodging a throng of young men, more soldiers, out for a night of fun. He caught up with Foxglove at the Plaza of the Rockies. Foxglove tried to hide behind a Humpty Dumpty sculpture, but his wide-brimmed cowboy hat gave him away.

"Give up," Thorne said, panting to catch his breath. "Where is your princess castle?"

Lance followed on Thorne's heels, still recording. Thorne had to resist the temptation to throttle Foxglove. A crowd was gathering, and people had their phones out. The last thing Thorne needed was to assault skinny Foxglove on camera.

One young man asked, "Isn't that the guy from the videos?"

"Sure is," said a guy with a Southern accent. "I owe every date I've ever had to him."

It seemed soldiers from nearby military bases were fans of

Foxglove's tutorials.

Foxglove stood up straight. He adjusted his red cowboy hat. "My fans often wish to know where my castle is, but that information is strictly confidential."

There were murmurs from the interested crowd.

"Tell me." Thorne took a step closer to him. "People are looking for Lovey Dearheart, and I think you know where she is."

"Lovey?" Foxglove gasped. "I honestly don't know."

Thorne balled his hands into fists and glared at Foxglove.

"I can't tell you where she is," Foxglove whined, "but I will tell you what I know. But not here." He looked around at the crowd, speaking loudly enough for even those at the outer edges to hear, "This is top secret information pertinent to an upcoming show. Subscribe to my podcast channel today to receive discounted early access to new episodes."

"You're going to film Lovey?" Thorne grimaced. "Doing what?"

"Come to my office," Foxglove said to Thorne. "Tomorrow."

Thorne wanted answers right now. But Foxglove held out a fist full of coupons. The military guys clamoring for a discount formed an impenetrable wall.

Learning more would have to wait.

# 24

# ❋ Brie ❋

When Brie walked into the dance class on Friday, the students were twittering with excitement.

"Have you seen him yet?" Diana asked the cookie lady. "I'm thinking of pulling a muscle on purpose, just so he can work on me."

"Oh, Diana," Layton scolded. "Don't be silly. It's not worth injuring yourself just to enjoy eye candy."

Diana flapped a hand in front of her face, as if she needed to cool herself. "You know I wouldn't do anything that rash just for a pretty face. But I might *fake* an injury."

"Here. Have some peanut brittle." The cookie lady held a dish toward Diana. "This might satisfy your sweet tooth."

Both senior women giggled. Brie wondered whether they were talking about Riggs for a moment, but everyone in class knew the policeman. And he didn't "work" on people. As a policeman, maybe he "worked over" criminals once in a while.

"Good morning, everyone." Brie felt optimistic.

Thanks to Brie's extra practice when she went home last night, she was feeling more confident about the dance than she ever had. She was almost excited to show the seniors her moves.

"Brie, I have a question," Layton said.

"Of course, Layton. What's on your mind?"

"Can that new physical therapist dance?" he asked.

*Oh. Diana and the cookie lady were talking about the new guy.* It was a little bit horrifying to realize the old women had been gushing over the young physical therapist's looks. Brie could admit he was a handsome guy. *But he's not as cute as Riggs.*

"If he knows how to bust a move," the cookie lady said, "maybe he could be our instructor. Until Lovey returns."

"That's what I've been doing," Brie said with dismay. "Filling in for Lovey. The Valentine's Showcase is tomorrow. It's too late to make drastic changes now."

"I don't want you old fools thinking my grandson is at your beck and call. However, I gave him permission to take over this class permanently," George said. "Riggs said he's too busy, but he really doesn't have any better way to spend his free time. I've almost given up on him finding the right girl to settle down with. The boy hasn't been on a date in forever and a day."

Brie tried not to look interested. But it sounded like Riggs didn't have a social life.

*Like me.*

"My grandson was a cheerleader in high school," George continued. "He has real-world experience performing for a crowd." He pulled out his cellphone. "I'm calling Riggs."

*But I'm right here,* Brie wanted to say.

The policeman must have been in the gym. He appeared moments later, and not in uniform. His workout clothes of a snug T-shirt and knee-length bicycle shorts showed every lean muscle. He was sweaty, and had a small towel draped across his shoulders.

"I was working out before my shift starts, Grandpa George. What do you need?"

"You're taking over this class."

"But Brie is the substitute instructor." Riggs shot a sheepish look her direction. "Aren't you?"

"She was," George said. "But we're firing that stoner and

hiring you."

"Grandpa, that's really rude. Brie has worked hard to learn the dance routine. She knows what she's doing now."

*He's standing up for me?* Brie's heart skipped a beat. She mouthed the words, "Thank you," to Riggs.

"She'll be great," Riggs said.

Sam Slate wrinkled their nose. "Brie, you're a dear to want to help, but your style is so different than what we're going for."

"I'm sorry," Layton said, "but I have to agree with Sam. Riggs, you really get it."

"We're out of time." Diana clasped her hands together as she addressed Riggs, looking like she was saying a silent prayer. "The Showcase is tomorrow. We're in desperate need of your help."

Brie blinked back tears, and hoped she could speak around the lump in her throat. "It's okay. You're right. Riggs, if you could take over the class, that would free me to do my actual job."

Brie slunk away from the classroom, with the joyful sounds of seniors having fun at her back.

She felt utterly defeated. Brie hadn't been able to find Lovey. She'd let the ninja steal Duchess from her without getting any answers to her questions. And she'd just been fired from a volunteer job.

*What volunteer ever got fired?*

# 25

## ✳ Thorne ✳

"Welcome, Mr. Bramble." Demetrius Foxglove shook Thorne's hand.

Thorne winced. Both of his arms ached. One from the dart that had pierced his trench coat sleeve, and the other from the tetanus shot he'd gotten at the urgent care facility. Thorne couldn't afford to get his winter trench coat dry cleaned and repaired yet. So he had switched to his black leather overcoat instead. It wasn't quite as warm, but it looked official enough.

Foxglove led him to a seat at a small glass-topped table, then sat across from Thorne.

"Can my assistant offer you anything to make you more comfortable? Coffee, perhaps? Donut?"

Foxglove's receptionist waved from her desk. "It's no trouble at all."

"Both will be fine. Thanks."

Thorne was still exhausted from the chase through downtown Colorado Springs last night and the trip to the emergency clinic. The least the guy could do for his troubles was give Thorne a free coffee and donut. He hoped the receptionist stocked sugary creamers. *The good kind.*

"Now, let's get down to business," Foxglove said. "Why were you chasing me?"

"Seriously?" Thorne asked Foxglove. "Why did *you* run from *me*? Where are you hiding her?"

"Hiding who?" Foxglove put his hands up. "Look, if your girlfriend or wife left you after talking to me, I can't help—"

"No! Don't be ridiculous!" Thorne said in exasperation. Although the man did have a way with women. "Don't play coy. I already told you, I'm a PI, and I've been hired to find Lovey Dearheart."

"So she really is missing?" Foxglove stood up with a level of shock that didn't seem like an act. He paced around the room on his long grasshopper legs. "No, no, no, no. What happened? This is terrible!"

The receptionist carried a tray to the table. On it were two cups of coffee and a plate of assorted donuts. *Ooh, and a bowl of individual creamers.* There was a nice variety of flavors to choose from.

"Now calm down, Mr. Foxglove," she said. "Have a seat. We can't have you spilling again. It's so expensive to get your nice suit dry cleaned."

"Oh come on, Mom!" Foxglove sat obediently despite his protest.

The woman gave Foxglove a stern look.

The skinny man pointed his eyes to the floor. "I mean, Mrs. Foxglove."

"Be sure to have a donut or two," the receptionist said. "You could stand to gain a few pounds, honey."

*Not the Godmother. Just Foxglove's regular mother.* She patted Foxglove's arm, then left the room.

"So you really don't know anything about Lovey's disappearance," Thorne said, skeptically.

Thorne eyed Foxglove for tells as he took a sip of coffee. He grimaced and forced himself to swallow. Foxglove's mom served a mean cup. Thorne opened one of each of the five flavors of creamer and dumped them into his coffee. *Suicide flavor.* It was better, but not quite there. Thorne opened five more creamers.

He wondered if a piece of peanut brittle would cut the astringent flavor. But if Foxglove saw it, Thorne might be forced to share. He took a big bite of a chocolate-frosted donut. *It's fresh. Wow.* The multi-colored sprinkles tumbled off, rolled across the table, and onto the floor. Thorne pushed them with the toe of his shoe under the table closer to Foxglove. *Maybe his mother will blame him for the mess instead.*

"I know about the letters you sent Lovey," Thorne said around a mouthful. "This won't look good to the police. Where are you keeping her?"

"You think I kidnapped Lovey?" Foxglove asked, clearly horrified.

"Right now, you look like a stalker. But it's not a big step from stalker to kidnapper."

"I'm a huge fan of hers, but I'm no stalker." Foxglove sipped his battery acid straight, with no creamer to dilute it. Thorne had to give it to him. The guy had moxie. He barely made a face as he swallowed. "My career was inspired by Lovey. She played the ideal woman on her show. And the men in the romance movies she introduced were the inspiration for who I am today. Having her guest star on my show was going to be a gamechanger for me. She could take my number of subscribers over the top. Get me monetized. Make me famous."

Judging by the reaction of the soldiers last night, Foxglove already seemed pretty famous by local standards, but where did Foxglove rank on the national stage?

Thorne considered the guy. It all fit and made sense. Old-time romance movies featured a lot of ideas that wouldn't be popular in today's social climate. Foxglove had tried to modernize the swaggering hero, with somewhat cringy results. Getting Lovey Dearheart on his show would do a lot for his channel.

"Well, Mr. Foxglove. It seems we have a shared goal. Do you have any ideas as to where Lovey might be now?" Thorne asked.

"Well, she was married three times. Her first husband left her a widow. She divorced the other two. They got married and live in California now."

"They started new families?"

"Family. The two men married each other. I follow them on social media. They have no interest in Lovey that I can tell, except for the alimony checks she sends them."

"That's gotta sting," Thorne said. His alimony checks went toward paying for his ex-wife Eden's travels in Tibet. His situation paled in comparison to what Lovey was going through.

"Lovey wasn't lucky in love, that's for sure." Foxglove bit into a maple-frosted donut and swallowed. "She has no children. Not even stepchildren. Her agent died ten years ago. Her mentor from when she was a Las Vegas showgirl lives in an Ohio nursing home. And—"

For a guy who wasn't stalking Lovey, he knew way too much about her personal life.

"Anybody you can think of that would mean Lovey harm?" Thorne interrupted.

"Maybe someone from Las Vegas? A former romantic rival, perhaps?" Foxglove suggested. "Though it seems like if they had a problem with her, they would have dealt with her long ago."

Thorne sighed. Another dead end.

Foxglove continued. "I don't have a clue."

Thorne sipped his still acrid, syrup textured coffee. "Neither do I."

# 26

# ✳ Lovey ✳

Friday, the Hoffmans settled in for a cozy evening watching television. Lovey enjoyed the fluff and fun of cheerful musicals as much as anyone, but she wondered whether a little variety might help them see the world in a more realistic manner. A nature documentary, perhaps. A competitive cooking program. A show about travel to an exotic location.

She would have time to suggest minor changes to a routine Harry and Sally clearly loved. She had signed the ninja's contract. Lovey was a part of the family now. She sighed with happiness as she cuddled Duchess in her lap, with Chrissy tucked at her side.

Randall stood, threw his arms above his head, and yawned. The stretching seemed a bit over the top for Lovey's discerning taste in acting.

"I'm going to study in my room," Randall said. "Before I fall asleep. I have a paper due Monday."

"You're really that tired?" Sally quirked an eyebrow. "It's only six o'clock."

Harry piped in, "You remember being a teenager, dear. Fourteen-year-olds need a lot of sleep. I know I did at his age."

Sally frowned, "Okay, Randy. Don't forget to brush your teeth." Her eyes followed her son until he left the room.

"You really think he's okay?" Sally asked Harry. "He's been acting even stranger than usual."

"Teenagers are strange." Harry chuckled.

"What do you think, Mom?" Sally asked Lovey.

*Mom.* Lovey smiled at the word. After resisting being called mother when she first arrived, Lovey embraced the title now. Years ago, she had given up on anyone ever applying the name to herself, and she relished every time she heard it. And now her *daughter* was seeking her advice.

"Maybe he just needs some space," Lovey suggested.

But Lovey wasn't as certain as she pretended to be. She might not have experience with raising children, but she recognized a sneaky look when she saw one. Randall slipped from the room like a thief.

Sally seemed satisfied by Lovey's answer and went back to watching the movie in earnest. Duchess stood up on Lovey's lap, walked in a circle, and curled back up into a ball to sleep.

Lovey tried to enjoy the movie, too, but thoughts of Randall wouldn't leave her be.

"You know what?" Lovey asked. "I'm exhausted."

She yawned in a much more realistic way. Duchess yawned and stretched, adding credence to Lovey's act. She lifted Duchess from her lap and set the dog on the floor.

Lovey stood. "I'm off to bed."

"Oh! Of course," Harry jumped to his feet. "Need any help?"

Everyone seemed ready to believe little old ladies required an early bedtime to function. Even though it was absurdly early.

"No need." Lovey tested out a new word. "Son. I know my way around." She smiled.

After going to her room, Lovey piled a row of pillows on her bed and threw the comforter over them. An old trick, but an effective one. Then she turned off the lights, lifted Duchess into her arms, and tiptoed down the hall to Randall's room. She tapped on the door.

*No answer.*

Lovey tried the doorknob. Locked. Why did modern parents allow their children to lock their bedroom doors? Maybe she was too old-fashioned for this world. At least the lock was low-tech, designed to deter being walked in on during an inconvenient moment, but not a serious preventative to entry.

A simple jab at the center of the doorknob with a hairpin was all it took. Lovey turned the knob and peeked inside. The bed looked like it contained a sleeping occupant, but Lovey wasn't fooled. She jerked back the quilt to expose a row of pillows.

*Great minds think alike.* As she suspected, Randall was gone. She stepped back into the hallway. Which means of exit had he taken?

At the end of the hallway, she heard a rustling sound coming from the attached garage. Lovey pressed her ear to the door. Duchess whined.

"Hush, girl. Don't give us away."

Lovey eased the door open. Randall rolled an all-black bicycle with spikes sticking out of the rims toward the sidewalk in front of the house. A long black coat wafted behind him in the wind. His thigh-high boots left tracks in the snow.

Modern garage doors were quiet. But Lovey was still surprised she hadn't heard it opening. She stepped inside and gently pulled the interior door closed. Duchess yipped softly.

"Uhhn!" Randall's face twisted with a repressed startled yell.

"What are you doing, young man?" Lovey whispered harshly.

He pressed one hand to his chest. "You scared me," he whispered back.

"You didn't answer my question."

Randall scrunched up his face, looking positively agonized. "I'm not doing anything bad. Actually, I'm going to school."

"At this hour?" Lovey asked. Randall told her the practices

for his high school skit were during his lunch hour at school. "What for? It's almost dark outside." Night came so early in the wintertime. "You can't go bike riding at night. What if you slip on a patch of ice?"

*And how can he possibly pedal wearing those boots?*

"Please let me go!" Randall looked frantic. "And you can't tell Mom and Dad."

What was going on in young Randall's life? Had he been placed in detention for some violation of school rules?

"Can't tell them what?" Lovey asked. "Randall, I'm part of this family now. I can't keep quiet if you're in some kind of trouble."

"Please. You have to let me leave." He waited, but Lovey gave him what she hoped was a glare heavy with grandparental authority. "It's the skit I told you about. Remember?"

"I'm not senile, young man. You told me your high school is performing at the Valentine's Showcase. Imagine my surprise when there was nothing on Tuesday's rehearsal schedule about *The Tell-Tale Heart*. Were you fibbing to me?"

"Fi- what?"

"Fabricating. Misrepresenting." She tried his teen lingo. "*Capping*?"

"No! Of course not!" Randall huffed out a breath that spread in the cold air in a foggy cloud. "All the outside acts got their time on stage that night," he said, "We're having our dress rehearsal tonight. Is seeing it on the school schedule proof enough for you?"

He pulled out his phone and clicked rapidly, then handed the device to Lovey. An official-looking calendar for Juniper Breeze High School listed the theater club's rehearsal this evening. Lovey handed him back the phone.

"I've kept your secret, but this has gone too far. It's not fair to surprise them like this. You have to tell your parents."

"They'll hate it. You know the story of Edgar Allen Poe's *The Tell-Tale Heart*. There are no musical numbers, and it's definitely scary."

Lovey debated for a moment. "Every parent should be proud of their children's accomplishments. They'll just have to get over it."

"I can't tell them tonight," Randall said. "They might ground me or tell my teacher I can't be in the skit. Please! I just need to get to rehearsal. The play is tomorrow. I don't have time for Mom and Dad to get over it. I'm playing the lead. I can't let everyone down."

"Randall, I cannot allow you to ride your bicycle all the way to your school in the dark and the cold."

Gusts of biting February wind pushed ice crystal-coated aspen leaves through the open garage door. Randall's shoulders slumped. He looked to be nearly in tears.

Lovey had learned enough from family movies that giving in to teenage temper tantrums was a bad idea. But this wasn't just a child being rebellious. This was really important.

"I'll drive you there."

Randall raced over to her and Duchess, wrapping them both in a hug. "Thank you, Grandma."

If his acceptance was designed to melt her heart, well . . . it worked. Lovey took the sedan's key fob off a hook on the neat key-shaped rack. Better to take the older vehicle without permission than attempt escape in the new minivan. Plus, she hadn't driven in a while, and it might be safer to take a smaller car.

Randall had the idea to push the sedan out of the garage. He hopped in, and they rolled backward down the sloping driveway past the family's trash and recycling barrels. Lovey started the car when they reached the street.

"I must ask," she said. "When you took the trash out tonight, did you deliberately leave the garage door open, in anticipation of this escapade?"

Randall grinned. "Yep."

"Devious." Lovey couldn't suppress her own grin.

The high school was bright with interior lights. Lovey took a seat in the nearly empty audience, placing Duchess on her lap.

The teacher seemed at ease with the barely contained chaos of the high school theater students. Lovey glanced at the analog clock on the wall. If correct, a dreadful amount of time was passing. She worried about the Hoffmans checking on her or their son.

The big moment finally came. Lovey watched the dress rehearsal while perched on the edge of her seat. Randall was frighteningly convincing as the crazy narrator. Harry and Sally had a very talented son.

After the play, Randall chattered happily. He was bursting with excitement. The normally stoic boy smiled from ear to ear all the way home. Lovey pulled the sedan into the garage. She turned off the ignition.

The garage door lowered behind the car. Lovey had not pushed the garage door button. Her normally healthy and reliable heart stuttered briefly. *Trapped!*

The Hoffmans burst through the door from the house.

"It's about time you got home," Harry said sternly. He looked at his cellphone screen. "It's past curfew for you, young man."

"Thank goodness you came back, Mom," Sally said. "When you and Randall vanished, we were worried to pieces that something terrible happened!"

*Worse than getting kidnapped by a ninja?*

"Where did you go?" Chrissy wailed. "Did you go get ice cream without me?"

Lovey looked at Randall. He clasped his hands together, with a pleading look in his eyes. She couldn't give away his harmless secret. Not while his parents were so angry.

*They'll learn the truth tomorrow.*

"We just went for a little drive," Lovey said.

Randall nodded his agreement. It wasn't factually untrue, but it was a lie of omission.

Harry threw the door to the house open wide. "Family conference time. Into the kitchen."

Lovey trudged down the hallway. Her poodle's claws skittered across the flooring in sync with Lovey's high heels.

"I am so disappointed," Harry said. "Why didn't you tell us you needed to go somewhere? We would have let you borrow a car. You're family. But sneaking around like this . . . It's—"

"It's just plain wrong." Sally's lower lip quivered.

The tension in the kitchen was unbearable. Until Sally pulled on a frilly apron and busied herself at the kitchen counter.

"This situation calls for hot cocoa." Sally spoke in a cheerful voice, but a quaver gave away her true emotion. "Marshmallows can cure any heartache."

"We— I brought the car back," Lovey said.

The young man did nothing to explain their unapproved absence, but perhaps his silence was for the best. She was ready to accept all the blame. Maybe if she hadn't taken the car and had let Randall ride his bike, his escape wouldn't have been discovered. *But what if he had crashed his bicycle into a frozen ditch? I did the right thing.*

"Our trial week isn't up yet," Harry said. "I'm no longer certain you're who we thought you were."

"Harry," Sally gasped.

"I signed the contract," Lovey said. "This is just a little misunderstanding."

"I'm calling the ninja." Harry walked to a cookie jar. He thrust his hand inside and retrieved a shiny black sphere.

Duchess barked at it. She probably thought they were going to play fetch. Lovey held the pink puppy snugly in her arms.

"Are you sure, darling?" Sally asked as she stirred cocoa into a pot of milk. "Can't we work this out on our own?"

"By golly, I just don't know what to do. We need a third party to mediate this situation," Harry said, clutching the sphere tightly. "Stand back!"

"Daddy, no!" Chrissy threw her arms around Lovey. "I love

this grandma!"

Randall leapt in front of Lovey and Chrissy with his arms spread wide. "No, Dad! Wait!"

Harry threw the black sphere at the floor. It burst into a cloud of smoke. The gray cloud slowly dissipated.

"What on Earth?" Lovey cried.

"That's supposed to bring her to our house," Sally said. "Where's the ninja?"

"Before, it worked just like Aladdin's lamp," Harry said. "Now I'm not so sure this Grandparent Placement service works as advertised."

"Where is this advertised?" Lovey asked. *And why hasn't it come to the attention of the authorities?*

"'Advertised' is the wrong word for it," Sally said. "Harry and I were on a date night. Ballroom dancing."

"We were doing zigzags in a foxtrot across the floor when I . . ." Harry looked embarrassed.

"He stepped on my foot." Sally smiled. "It was more surprising than painful. Harry is a wonderful dancer. It was all my fault. I tripped him up."

"I'm not as graceful as you, dear." Harry made moon-eyes at Sally. "Anyway, we went to sit down near a water station. I think I said something about wishing my father was a podiatrist instead of a proctologist. Then he could have helped if Sally's foot was really injured."

"I said, if my mother were a dancer, maybe I wouldn't have tripped Harry up in the first place."

"Then we both wished out loud that any of our parents would take an interest in our lives—" Sally choked up. Through sobs, she said, "Or our children's. We both made the wish for a grandparent at the same time."

Harry took her in his arms. "Later that evening, I found one of those black spheres in my jacket pocket with a card that said, 'Make your wishes come true by throwing this sphere.'"

"We threw it," Sally said. "When the smoke cleared, there

was a ninja standing in our living room."

Harry grabbed the contract and waved it near Lovey. "We'll settle this if and when she finally shows up. There has to be an equitable solution."

Duchess strained in Lovey's arms. With all the tears and excitement, the pink poodle had reached her maximum stress level. She snapped with her fuzzy muzzle and grabbed the contract in her teeth. Harry held on. They played tug-of-war for a moment before the kitchen was filled with the sound of tearing parchment.

Harry stared at the half-contract in his hand with an expression of horror. "What have I done?"

"Does that void the contract?" Sally asked in a hoarse whisper.

"That paper looks really old," Randall said with trembling lips. "Like it's magical or something."

Lovey would like to believe there was magic left in this sad old world.

"You broke the magic spell!" Chrissy stomped her little feet across the kitchen floor and stood looking up at her father. "You're going to make my Grandma go away!" Then she burst into tears and hugged onto Harry's legs.

Harry and Lovey said in unison, "What do we do now?"

"This hot cocoa isn't going to drink itself," Sally said with a strained smile. As she ladled the steaming beverage into mugs, she burst into song. "The sun will come out, tomorrow!"

The rest of the family joined in, singing through their tears.

# 27

# ✳ Brie ✳

Brie had a Saturday off for a change. It rarely worked out that way, but it was nice when it happened. She had slept in, cleaned house, and made herself a nice breakfast of French toast and a spinach omelet.

She still felt surprisingly bitter about getting "fired" yesterday. But did it matter who filled in now to do the job when it was supposed to be Lovey? The senior was still missing. Had Brie done enough for her? *No. I haven't.*

Even though Riggs had called the Ripped Bodice Romance convention without results, Brie had to give it a shot. Her call only resulted in being scolded for attempting to violate attendee privacy. Calling back a second time, and disguising her voice, pretending to be Lovey's niece, earned her an actual threat of a police report.

Driving to Denver to search the convention in person might have been her next move, if not for the ominous weather forecast. A major winter storm threatened to hit the Mile High City just in time for Valentine's Day. Fortunately, Colorado Springs was only expected to get a dusting of snow. *As if anyone can accurately predict the weather in the foothills below Pikes Peak.*

She clutched the red sparkly flower that used to adorn

Duchess in one hand. In the other, she held the tissue-wrapped hilt of the kunai knife. It was so sharp. She hunted around for something to put it in. Brie got the hard purple plastic case labeled "girly stuff" she kept in her purse. She nestled the knife and the rosette in between the feminine hygiene products and snapped the lid shut. The two items were the strongest leads to Lovey she had.

Brie's father wasn't making any progress. And Barry was being evasive about the whole ninja thing. Why should Brie trust someone who dressed up like a ninja, broke into her home, and stole purse puppies? She needed advice from a professional.

Brie took Rigg's card from her purse. She took a deep breath and dialed. She almost hung up after the fourth ring. But he answered.

"Officer Saito speaking," Riggs said.

Brie froze up.

"Hello?" Riggs sounded annoyed.

"Um, hi. This is Brie. You know, from the HMCA."

"Brie, of course!" His voice softened.

"I was wondering if you want to meet for bubble drinks today," Brie said.

"Bubble drinks? Like champagne?"

Brie smiled. Riggs seemed like he was prematurely old sometimes.

"No. I probably should have said 'bubble tea' instead. Have you ever had Thai milk tea?"

Brie was cultured enough to know Saito was a Japanese surname. It would be wrong to assume he liked Thai food. She knew from personal experiences that cultural stereotypes could be hurtful. *After all, I'm not a big fan of watermelon.*

"Yeah. Thai tea is delicious," Riggs said.

"Bubble teas are just drinks like that with big tapioca balls in them called boba."

"That sounds interesting. This is my work phone, but I'm not on duty for a couple of hours. Let me give you my personal number so you can text me the address."

"Great!" *He's giving me his personal number?* Brie tried not to read too much into it.

He hung up before she could ask him to bring a fingerprint kit. He could always take the knife back to the station for processing. She still hadn't touched the knife without covering her hands first. *Hopefully, my handling of the kunai with tissues hasn't wiped off any evidence.*

A couple of hours later, Brie walked into Kawaii Bubbles Tea House and realized her mistake. The usually cute anime-themed drink place had been transformed. Red garlands coated in hearts were strung across the ceiling. Several bouquets of fake roses adorned the ordering counter. Each small table was covered with a pink tablecloth. Goo-goo eyed couples shared drinks at many of the tables. Brie looked at her phone calendar.

*Valentine's Day.*

"Hi, Brie," Riggs said from behind her. He must have just walked in.

Brie spun around and looked up at him. He was dressed in slacks and a button-up shirt. Brie had on faded black workout leggings and an old University of Colorado at Colorado Springs sweatshirt with frayed cuffs and a grease stain that never came out, no matter what she did. No makeup, hair in its usual messy puff ponytail on the back of her head. Riggs looked ready for a date. Brie looked like a disaster.

But surely he didn't dress up like this for her. Maybe he had an actual date planned after this.

"Hello, Riggs," Brie said.

"I'm glad you called me. I'm kind of bad about these things. I never know when it's the right time to ask."

*Ask what?* Brie had no idea what he was talking about. She called him to pick his brain about Lovey's disappearance. *What did he think this was about?*

"I have a lot of questions, too. There's so much to talk about. Wanna get some tea first?"

"Yes," Riggs said. "It smells so good in here."

Riggs ordered a Thai tea with brown sugar boba. Brie got taro milk tea with lychee. She wasn't sure if she cared for taro flavor, but she always ordered it because the root vegetable drink was a pretty shade of lavender.

Riggs started to pull the plastic seal off the top of his cup. Brie put a hand over his to stop him. "Not like that!"

Riggs looked from Brie's hand on top of his and up into her eyes. Brie swallowed and pulled her hand away. It felt so cold after touching his.

"Let me show you." She unwrapped Riggs's big straw and gripped it firmly. "You have to stab it in there." In one quick movement, she forced the pointy end of the straw through the plastic lid. She handed him his drink.

"Thanks." Riggs didn't take his eyes off her as he took a sip.

Brie stabbed her own straw into her taro milk tea and hesitated. He was still watching her.

"Aw! I think you guys are the cutest couple I've seen all day," a barista with a towel said as she wiped down the empty table next to Brie and Riggs.

Riggs gave Brie a big smile.

"Oh, we're not on a date," Brie blurted out to the barista.

Riggs's smile faded. Did he think this was a date? *Oh no! What have I done?*

"Sorry," Brie said. "I didn't realize it was Valentine's Day when I called you."

"Oh, I uh," Riggs said. They would probably both have turned bright red if their complexions did that sort of thing. Riggs pasted on an uncomfortable-looking grin with obvious effort. "It's fine. You didn't say anything about a date. I just made an assumption, and you know how that goes. What did you want to see me about?"

*Yikes!* Brie had dreamed of going on a date with Riggs. *And now I shut down my one chance. This might be the biggest fail of my entire life.*

"Is this about the Valentine's Showcase?" Riggs asked. "I didn't mean to take over like that. If you want to lead the seniors tonight—"

"No! It's not that," Brie cut him off. She hesitated for only a moment. "I can't keep this to myself any longer. A ninja came to my house to get Lovey's dog and return it to her." The words coming out of Brie's mouth sounded stupid to her own ears. "Lovey was supposed to be at the theater during the dress rehearsal. Maybe she was, but then she left. I just know she got her dog back, because I found the collar flower I showed you and your grandfather. So Lovey must be all right."

"That makes no sense at all," Riggs said.

"What do you have to say about this?" Brie pulled out the purple plastic "girly stuff" case, noticing too late the embarrassed look on Riggs's face. She snapped it open and pulled out the kunai knife. "I only know about ninjas from anime, like Naruto."

Riggs reached for the tissue-wrapped knife.

"Careful," Brie said. "There might be fingerprints. Although the ninja wore gloves."

"This isn't the first time you've brought up ninjas. They were part of the royal guard in Japan hundreds of years ago. And there are still real ninjas around today." He took a napkin from the dispenser on the table and used it to pick up the blade. He unwrapped it and handled the knife carefully with his napkin-covered hands. Riggs had turned off his playful date mode and was back to his all-business cop self. "You said you had a ninja in your home?"

"Yes. The ninja broke into my house and took Duchess, Lovey's dog."

"What were you doing with Ms. Dearheart's dog?"

*Great, he probably thinks I'm a thief now.* Brie looked away, unable to meet his eyes even when telling a little white lie. "I was dog-sitting while she's supposedly at the romance convention. And now her dog is gone, too."

"Why didn't you report the break-in?"

"The ninja said she was bringing the dog to Lovey," Brie explained.

"She?"

"The ninja is female, as far as I can tell."

"Were there any damages to your property?" Riggs asked.

"It's not my property. I live at my mom's house. Not with my mom, though." Riggs raised one of his perfect black eyebrows as Brie fumbled through her explanation. "It's a long story. But the house is fine. The knife only went through a box of tissues."

"It must be very sharp."

Brie nodded, hopeful he was finally taking her seriously. "Do you have a fingerprint kit? Maybe the ninja handled the knife before she put on gloves."

"Our evidence techs typically dust for prints," Riggs said. "You'd need to take this to the station. Report the break-in. It would have been better to leave the knife in place. There's a chain of custody problem now."

"Oh. I don't know if I want to go through all that."

"If you don't want to make an official report, and you and the seniors refuse to report Lovey missing, why did you call? What do you want from me?"

Brie was on the verge of tears. "I just wanted someone to talk to." *Wow, that sounded lonely and pathetic.* She sniffled. "I'm really sorry."

"Hey, don't cry." Riggs patted Brie's shoulder. "Here. I got you this."

He handed Brie a big red envelope. It had to be a Valentine. She held it so tight, she crumpled the side.

"I have to go," Brie said. She couldn't bear one more moment of this. How could she have screwed things up so badly with such a nice guy? "I'll open it later."

She grabbed the kunai knife with her bare hand and shoved it inside the "girly stuff" case. She dropped it and the card into her purse.

Brie realized a moment too late that if there had been any fingerprints on the kunai, they were ruined now.

# 28

# ✷ Lovey ✷

Harry offered Lovey a heart-shaped biscuit. They were so delicious with strawberry jam. The perfect addition to the Valentine's Day lunch the Hoffmans prepared.

"The ninja must have come last night," Sally said, "but she didn't speak to us. Instead, we found the contract on the kitchen table this morning."

Sally held up the rice paper scroll. When Lovey went to bed last night, one torn half of the contract sat ominously on the kitchen counter. The other half had been crumpled and ravaged with holes from Duchess's tiny teeth. Chrissy tried to tape it together, but it refused to be mended. There was something special about it, as though it resisted the girl's efforts to fix the paper. This morning, the two pieces had been mended back together. Lovey saw no tape or glue. No doggy teeth marks. *Must be ninja magic.*

The parchment was still tattered. Even though now there were no signatures, this was clearly the original contract. It appeared the ink had been erased. No, it was more like the signatures had never been there.

Lovey's heart skipped a beat. "The contract has been repaired? What happened to our names? What do you think it means?"

"We think the ninja was trying to send us a message," Harry said. "We have to sign it again for us to become a real family?" He shrugged.

"I think it means we should give this whole thing a second chance," Sally said.

"A do-over?" Chrissy asked, her eyes pleading.

The young girl squeezed Lovey's hand. Lovey returned the squeeze.

"I want to stay," Lovey said. "But I understand if you don't want me to. I crossed a line. I took your car and your child without permission. I'd be upset, too."

"It's all water under the bridge," Harry said. "We've forgiven you."

"Do you forgive us for overreacting?" Sally asked.

"Of course! But now I'm worried about the ninja. Is becoming a family up to us? How much power does the ninja have over this whole situation?"

Even though they had made up, the unsigned contract left them all solemn on what should be the happiest day of the year: Valentine's Day.

"I know one thing that will lift everyone's mood," Sally said.

Harry nodded, as though he could read his wife's mind. "Well," Harry asked, "what are we waiting for? Let's sign this!"

They pulled out the raven's feather and pot of ink. Harry moved the ink-dipped tip over the parchment in a flourish. The paper stayed blank.

"Huh," Harry said.

"Let's see if the quill is working." Lovey took the feather. "Do you have another piece of paper?"

Sally set a shopping list pad in front of Lovey who dragged the quill across the paper. Black ink coiled across the yellow, checkered pad in Lovey's lacy signature.

"It's not the quill." Lovey dipped the feather in ink again, and scrawled across the parchment. It was like trying to sign waxed paper. The parchment rejected the ink. "What's wrong with it?"

Lovey's sunny optimism wavered. She feared the reason the contract didn't work was because she had failed at her only chance to become part of this family.

"What if the ninja is busy finding a different senior citizen to be your grandparent? Maybe that's why we can't sign the contract now."

"No way!" Chrissy exclaimed. "You're the only grandma I want!"

"Maybe the problem is that we need the whole family here," Harry said. "Ninja magic?"

Lovey didn't believe the black-garbed woman who kidnapped her was a supernatural being. But there was so much about this she couldn't explain.

"Ninja magic!" Sally exclaimed. "Harry, you're brilliant! We need Randy."

"My brother sleeps forever on the weekends." Chrissy made an adorable pouting face. "I'll go wake him up." She dashed to Randall's room.

Lovey let her heart hope this was the solution to signing the contract. While she waited for Chrissy to bring Randall to the kitchen, Lovey bit into another fluffy biscuit. *Delightful!* It was like taking a bite out of love itself. Butter and strawberry jam leaked from the corners of her mouth. She dabbed at her face with a lacey cloth napkin.

Chrissy ran back into the kitchen. "Randy's not in his room!"

"Where is he?" Sally cast a curious look at Lovey.

"I have nothing to do with his disappearance this time." Lovey had been in her room all morning. She had been waiting in dread, afraid the act of tearing the contract and summoning the ninja meant Lovey was in danger of being whisked away from the people she so badly wanted to call family.

Harry jumped up so fast that he almost knocked his chair

over. He ran down the hall to the garage.

"His bicycle is missing!" Harry yelled.

Sally stared at her phone screen. "We should be able to track him from his phone, but the Where is My Family app isn't showing where he is. He must have disabled it."

"We only installed it for safety, not to invade each other's privacy. But now this?" Harry huffed. "We were too trusting. Randy's completely out of line." He turned to Lovey and pleaded, "What are we going to do?"

"Calm down. I think I know where he is," Lovey said. "Let's go."

"Where?" Sally asked.

"To the high school."

"Randy went to school early on a Saturday?" Chrissy crinkled her nose in disgust.

"Are you sure? We still have plenty of time before we have to leave for the Valentine's Showcase," Harry said. "Why didn't he wait so we could all go together?"

"He has his reasons," Lovey said. "Randall will just have to explain it himself."

The family piled into the minivan with the contract rolled up like a scroll in Sally's purse, and drove toward Juniper Breeze High School. Chrissy sat next to Lovey and put her small hand in hers. Lovey focused on the warmth. She needed this.

"Grandma? Why are teenagers like this?"

"It's all part of growing up. When you're Randall's age, you might have something important to you that the rest of us don't understand. You might even break the rules too, sometimes."

"Me? Never!" Chrissy looked thoughtful, then asked. "Is growing up why he doesn't want to be called Randy anymore? Do you think he's breaking rules because we keep calling him Randy?"

"That might be a tiny part of it. He's trying to find his own identity. What he wants to be called is part of how he defines himself to others."

"Randall is my father's name," Harry said. "I'm surprised Randy wants to use it. He hates proctology. My given name is Harold, but that's too formal for a guy like me."

"I like that all our nicknames end in the letter 'Y,'" Chrissy said. "Even yours, Grandma." Chrissy stared at Lovey with adoring eyes. "My real name is really Christina. I like it. Maybe I'll use it when I'm a grumpy teenager. Is Lovey the name you were born with?"

"No, but it is the name I've gone by for fifty years," Lovey said.

"What was your birth name?" Sally asked.

Chrissy piped in, "Mom! Wait! Randy said I shouldn't ask people what their 'dead names' are."

"Dead names?" Harry asked.

"I think my brother wants 'Randy' to be his dead name," Chrissy said. "He wants us to call him Randall, so I guess we shouldn't call him Randy anymore."

*Dead names?* The idea fit. Lovey's birth name was from another life.

"I don't mind telling you mine," Lovey said. She squeezed Chrissy's hand. "My birth name was Myrna."

Chrissy made an expression like she smelled something unpleasant.

Lovey laughed. "Yeah. That's what I thought, too. But it actually means 'beloved.'"

"Oh," Chrissy said. "So you didn't really change your name that much."

"Right."

"Mom," Harry said as he took a corner so fast the tires squeaked on the pavement, "I think we overreacted last night."

"We need you in our family," Sally said. "Our parents are absent from our lives, by choice, or . . ." She paused, gazing out the window as they drove past a cemetery, bleak under the coating of winter snow. The woman clearly missed her father. "Having you with us these past few days made me realize how badly I miss my parents. Facetiming with my mother isn't the same as seeing her in person. Lichtenstein is so far away."

Lovey watched a tear leak down Sally's cheek. She blinked back her own.

"I have fond memories of my grandfather," Harry said. "It was a precious relationship. To see my kids missing out on interaction with that generation, well, it hurts. Grandparents are essential to a child's development. Just like having a mother is essential for Sally." He swallowed hard. "And me."

Lovey patted Chrissy's hand. "I've never experienced parenting or having grandchildren. I didn't know there was a hole in my heart that you all have filled."

Harry and Sally were silent as they pulled up to Juniper Breeze High School. Two dozen cars were already in the parking lot.

They unloaded the costumes, makeup, and props they needed for their routine and walked to the entrance.

"I didn't know the Showcase was going to be filmed." Harry pointed to a white guy with a messy copper-colored man bun. He was weighed down with heavy equipment. A full-sized tripod and a professional-grade camera were balanced awkwardly in his arms.

Harry dashed ahead and held the door for the man with the camera.

"Thanks, dude," the red-haired man mumbled. He shot a look at Lovey. Did he recognize her from TV? People usually didn't anymore, thanks to her advancing age, but she still had some diehard fans.

"Lovey Dearheart?" the guy asked.

There was no use denying her identity.

"Because every love story needs a happily ever after," Lovey quoted herself. She said those very words at the end of every episode of her show.

"Wow! I know someone who'd love an autograph. But my hands are full. Can I get one later?"

"Of course," Lovey said.

"My grandma is a celebrity!" Chrissy beamed.

The unsigned contract peeking out of Sally's purse made Lovey nervous. If the family didn't accept Randall's skit, Harry and Sally might blame Lovey for encouraging his rebellion. And Randall would never forgive Lovey for exposing his theatrical secret before the performance.

Lovey would never forgive *herself* if this family were torn apart by deceit. She had a sinking feeling that even ninja magic couldn't repair a rift that deep.

# 29

# ✳ Thorne ✳

Thorne's stomach still felt sour from the mostly creamer acid-coffee he drank at Foxglove's on Friday. It couldn't have been the three donuts he ate, or last night's dinner of several-days-old Angus Assistant leftovers. It was lunchtime, but Thorne wasn't feeling it. He nibbled on a piece of peanut brittle with his reheated Saturday morning coffee to try to settle his digestion.

He might not get any more of the sweet treat if he didn't find Lovey. The case was looking bleak.

He was certain the romance convention was a red herring. The Love Parlor had led to a dead end. Thorne rubbed his aching biceps. *And injuries.* If Foxglove didn't have Lovey locked up in his twisted castle of geriatric princesses, what kind of horrible situation could the old lady be in?

Thorne gave up on the medicinal properties of candy and popped an antacid tablet into his mouth. As he chewed the chalky pill, he realized he should give up trying to solve Lovey's case on his own. She could be in serious danger.

Defeat. Thorne didn't like to admit to it, but the consequences of not finding Lovey after so many days could be deadly.

He picked up his phone and called the police department. After speaking to the dispatcher, his call was transferred to an officer. Thorne could hear traffic noise in the background.

"Officer Riggs Saito. How may I help you?"

*Argh! Not that guy!*

Thorne had already swallowed his pride by calling the police. This was just one more blow against his PI ego.

"Hey, Officer. This is Thorne. From the HMCA." Those hints didn't seem to work. "Brie's father?"

"Oh, yes. Hello, Mr. Bramble. Hey, about earlier. I hope Brie wasn't upset about our little misunderstanding."

"You saw Brie today?" Thorne asked.

"Um, I thought . . . That's not what you're calling about. Of course." Riggs cleared his throat. "So, Mr. Bramble. What can I do for you?"

Thorne's phone buzzed with the notice that he had an incoming call. "Hang on a sec. I gotta see who's calling me."

"But you called me—"

Thorne cut Riggs off as he switched to the new call.

*Foxglove!*

"What do you want?" Thorne asked. Still flustered from his odd conversation with Riggs, he was perhaps a little abrupt, but Thorne was getting annoyed. Did Foxglove think they were friends now?

"Mr. Bramble, my videographer, Lance, was hired to film an event for livestreaming to the Juniper Breeze High School's social media channel."

"So?"

Foxglove had reached a new low, filming high school kids for his show. Thorne really had something to report to Officer Saito now!

"Imagine my surprise!" Foxglove exclaimed. "Lance called to tell me Lovey Dearheart just pulled into the parking lot."

"What?" Thorne couldn't believe his ears.

"I found her!" Foxglove said. "Who knows how long she'll be there. If we want to talk to her, we have to hurry."

"Where—" Thorne's phone buzzed with an incoming text

from Foxglove. The address of the high school. "Okay, I'll head there now."

"Can you swing by and give me a ride?" Foxglove asked. "Lance took the company van. Mom, I mean Mrs. Foxglove, is using her car today. And I just missed the bus . . ."

*Sheesh. This guy . . .*

"I guess—" Thorne started.

"I'll be waiting at the curb outside the Love Parlor."

Thorne stared at his phone after Foxglove hung up. *The nerve!*

"Hello?" Officer Saito asked.

Thorne's other call. *Oh yeah.* Riggs was still on the other line. "Never mind." He hung up and hurried to grab his keys.

*Foxglove is so annoying.* A total amateur had completed the job Thorne was hired to do. Well, not Foxglove, actually. That so-called Sir Lancelot guy was the one who located Lovey.

Thorne tried to ignore his frustration. He'd have all the answers soon. If he could reach the high school before Lovey disappeared again.

# 30

# ✳ Brie ✳

The morning "date" at the bubble drink shop could have sent Brie into a downward spiral of humiliation and despair. *No. Not this time*. Brie couldn't waste a rare Saturday off from her HMCA job to wallow in self-pity. She had another job to do. *Find Lovey.*

Brie wasn't giving up yet. She took the kunai knife to the only place in town she knew about that might help her. The Deepest Cut was a large store she'd never been inside of at the Citadel Mall. It was full of knives and swords. They might be able to tell her who bought this blade if it came from them. It was a long shot, but she had to do something to distract herself from her wounded feelings.

A heavy man wearing a too-small T-shirt and tattoo-covered arms stood behind the glass display case. His shirt read "Papa Bear," and had a realistic image of a grizzly bear growling and waving its claws. His brown hair hung limply to his shoulders, and a big beard covered most of his pale white face.

"Good afternoon, I'm Papa Bear," he said.

*I could have guessed that.*

"How can I help you?" he asked.

Brie turned her back to the guy while she removed the kunai knife from the hard plastic "girly stuff" case inside her old purse.

She placed it on the glass display case. The razor-sharp blade was as beautiful as it was potentially deadly. Striped patterns made the Damascus steel blade appear deceptively delicate. The short, black-wrapped handle might seem stubby, but was perfect for the purpose Brie had read about on the internet. They were usually flicked at opponents, not tissue boxes. Before she could even speak, the man gasped.

"Any student of Tommy Tigerclaw is always welcome in my shop," Papa Bear said with a bow. "It will be my honor to serve you."

*Tommy Tigerclaw?* Brie remembered Marty making a big deal of the rare martial arts VHS tapes he collected. There was a movie poster at the high school. Even her father had mentioned the guy. The Tigerclaw dude must be a real person.

"Do you have more of these?" Brie asked, pointing at the kunai blade.

The man lifted it into his hands like he was holding a rare relic. He studied it from all angles, then returned it to the display case top.

"This is one of the finest kunai blades I have ever seen," Papa Bear said.

He dashed around the display case and yanked the barred gate to his shop closed, locking Brie in and other potential customers out. Brie felt in her purse for the new container of pepper spray for whatever good that would do. She was locked in a shop full of sharp weapons with a guy who probably knew how to use them.

"My private collection is in the back."

"Whoa! I just wanted to know if this blade came from your shop," Brie said. "I'm looking for the owner. They left it at my house."

"Oh. I see." Papa Bear pulled his lips to one side in an annoyed expression, then reopened his shop.

*I guess I'm not going to get to see his "private collection,"* Brie thought with mild relief. Though now she was extremely curious.

"Can you tell me who bought this?" Brie asked.

"That particular blade didn't come from my shop, but I know the artist who made it," Papa Bear said with a tinge of regret. "Only the most secretive of people come here to buy these types of martial arts knives. They pay in cash, they leave no names, and they have no faces, if you catch my drift."

Brie didn't catch his drift, but she nodded anyway.

"You said something about Tommy Tigerclaw students?" Brie asked. "Do you have like a list or something?" At his blank stare, Brie added, "Where is the school?"

"If you were a student, you would know. Who are you, really? And what do you want?"

"I told you," Brie said, "I'm looking for the owner of this knife."

"You need to leave." Papa Bear pressed his large hands together, cracking his knuckles loudly. "Unless . . ."

"Yes?"

"Do you want to buy a truck?"

"Um." Brie looked around the shop. There were definitely no trucks in the store.

"Not here. At my house. I sell gently used trucks of all kinds. I even have a few Broncos."

"Oh!" Brie shook her head. She didn't need a truck, and she didn't need a horse. *Or a football player.* "No, thank you."

Brie tucked the kunai back into the purple case in her purse, and scuttled out of the shop into the mall.

*What was that about?* She hadn't learned the ninja's identity, but Papa Bear confirmed that there was a ninja school. *Maybe it's right here in Colorado Springs.*

A lot of athletes came to train in the high-altitude climate of the mountain city. The Olympic Training Center was only a couple of miles away from the mall Brie was standing in. None of this information got Brie closer to finding Lovey, but perhaps it was a good lead for learning more about the ninja that broke into her home.

The comforting, yeasty scent of freshly baked pretzels drew her down a hallway, and hopefully to safety. Her conversation with Papa Bear shook her to her very core. Her gut was screaming danger to her. *Or am I just hungry?* Before she could order one of the huge, salt-crusted twists of baked dough, her phone rang.

"Hello, Brie?" Riggs said through the phone.

Brie couldn't believe her ears. *He's actually calling me after what I did this morning?*

"Yes?" she asked hopefully. Maybe he called to ask her on a make-up date.

"Do you know where your father is?" he asked.

*Ugh!*

"Why would I—" Brie started. Her phone pinged. "Uh, hang on a second. He just texted me." Brie read her phone screen. She was so startled, she blurted out the news to the police officer. "He's on his way to Juniper Breeze High School. He found Lovey Dearheart! She showed up for the Valentine's Showcase like we hoped."

"We need to get over there. Fast!" Riggs said. "I can drive. Where are you?"

"I'm at the Citadel Mall."

"I'm in my patrol vehicle. I'll pick you up."

"Wait, Riggs," Brie said.

"Yes?" Riggs asked.

"Can I ride in the front seat this time?"

# 31

## ❈ Lovey ❈

"What's this?" Harry stabbed a finger against a poster on a sandwich board in the hallway outside the theater.

The Valentine's Showcase was advertised, with a large red arrow pointing toward the high school theater. Below a listing of the acts, including the Hoffman family, was a heart image that was not typical Valentine's decor. It resembled an actual human heart, with blood dripping from bulging veins. "*The Tell-Tale Heart, Abridged*, adapted from the short story by Edgar Allen Poe," was printed in gothic style font. The names and roles of the actors were listed.

"Randall Hoffman," Harry read, shaking his head.

"I don't understand," Sally said.

Lovey glanced around, catching a glimpse of Randall as he peeked out from a hallway. His eyes grew large as saucers. He held a finger to his lips, then he ducked away.

The secret was out. There was no need for Lovey to be silent any longer.

"Your son is the star of the high school skit," Lovey said with pride. *My grandson. I hope.*

Randall's name was in bold print. His role: Narrator.

"Ick." Chrissy grabbed onto her mother's arm. "Valentine's Day is about pink glittery hearts, not yukky blood and guts."

Randall needed his family's support, not criticism. She had

to admit the young man was not helping himself with his sneaky behavior.

*And by staying silent, I've been complicit in the lie.* Lovey wanted nothing more than to escape this tense situation. But not at the cost of a future with these caring people. This might be their last chance at healing. *If that parchment contract could be repaired, I have to believe this family can be, too.*

"Give your son a chance," Lovey said. She hugged Duchess close, needing the comfort of her little friend under these trying circumstances. "This is his big moment. You've given him his great love of theater. Perhaps this isn't your idea of entertainment, but he desperately wants your approval."

Sally clutched Chrissy's hand in hers. "The world is a scary place. That's why we prefer uplifting entertainment. Why does Randy, I mean Randall, have to betray everything we've taught him to be in this?" She waved a hand at the bloody poster.

"Because Randall is being disobedient," Harry said. "A rebellious teenager. Gosh darn it, he left the house without our permission. Twice!"

"Valentine's Day is about love," Lovey said. "Here's your chance to show that love to Randall."

"We changed our entire routine to accommodate your—" Sally paused, then added, "request."

"Now he's going to get to be in two shows," Chrissy said. "That's not fair."

"Let's focus on the Hoffman Family skit," Lovey said. "Randall will be there for you." She studied Harry and Sally's uncharacteristically stern faces. "Can you be there for him?"

The parents' expressions softened.

"Of course we will," Harry said. "That's what family is all about."

"Right! Come on," Sally said. "We need to put on our costumes."

The Hoffman family hurried to a classroom reserved as a dressing room. The last time Lovey was left alone, she had attempted to escape.

This time, she went down the hallway to the theater. She patted Duchess.

The seats slowly filled with attendees. The time for the Valentine's Showcase quickly approached. Lovey scanned the theater for her HMCA dance class. She was looking forward to seeing her students and introducing them to her new family. She'd never be able to explain the real reason she had been missing. *I sure hope they practiced.* A terrible thought occurred to her. Without her guidance, had they given up on the idea of performing in public? *Where are they?*

The theater doors burst open. A uniformed policeman walked in with long strides. *George's grandson.* Brie followed close behind. Lovey waved, but they must not have seen her. They ducked from the theater to a hallway.

A few moments later, two more people Lovey recognized entered the theater. Thorne Bramble sauntered in wearing one of his cute PI outfits. The man was adorable when he was flustered, but much too young for Lovey to actually pursue.

Lovey clutched Duchess tighter when she saw Thorne's traveling companion. *Demetrius Foxglove!* The annoying young man who had been spamming her email and snail mail for months with his ridiculous requests. As if she would help him in his pursuit of princesses to populate his disreputable castle. Hopefully, he wouldn't see her inside the dim theater. She ducked low in her seat and tried to hide behind Duchess.

The curtains fluttered as the singers, dancers, actors, and stagehands peeked out at the growing audience. Lovey thought it was cute, seeing performers checking to make sure their friends and family were arriving for the Showcase.

Lovey had done the same thing during her Vegas years, despite constant disappointment. The only ones ever waiting for her in the audience were gangster boyfriends or creepy fans.

Her life had certainly changed for the better. *If my new life with this family survives the Showcase.*

"Mom." Sally waved from the aisle. "Thanks for saving us seats. We don't go on until after several more acts."

Sally, Harry, and Chrissy all donned matching yellow rain jackets and hats. Their umbrellas were closed, and their rubber galoshes squeaked against the theater floor.

"We want to watch the other performances," Harry said.

Chrissy crossed her arms over her chest. "We looked and looked, but we couldn't find my brother." Chrissy suddenly perked up and pointed at the stage. "Look!"

Randall's face appeared briefly through the gap in the curtains. His lips formed an O of shock, and his face went even more pale than the stage makeup that aged him. A red vest contrasted with his gray Victorian suit. His black hair was slicked back and shiny.

"Randall!" Harry yelled. "We need to talk."

Lovey saw Randall tuck himself behind the curtain as quick as a flash.

"Randall," a teacher cried. "Randall! Where are you going? The skit is starting soon!"

Lovey saw Randall open a side door and race out of the theater into a hallway.

"Where's he going? He can't just leave before his big moment!" Chrissy cried. "He's the star!"

"He's afraid of what you'll say," Lovey said, standing up with Duchess in her arms. "Come on. The only thing that's going to fix this is the love of his family."

"Golly gee," Sally said. "We've certainly made a mess of things."

"What my brother needs is a biiiiiggg hug!" Chrissy stretched her arms wide.

Harry set his jaw with determination. "Sally, let's go get our boy."

Sally pumped her fist. "The show must go on."

# 32

# ❋ Brie ❋

After looking for Lovey in the hallways and backstage, Brie and Riggs returned to the seating area to continue their search.

"There's Lovey." Brie pointed across the rows of folding seats in the dark theater. "I told you she was safe."

"Then why is she running?" Riggs exclaimed.

Brie and Riggs dashed back out of the theater to catch up with Lovey. The white-haired woman was racing down a hallway with little pink Duchess trotting by her side. The dog's painted toenails clicked on the waxed floor. Lovey was faster than Brie expected an old lady to be, but she managed to catch up to her.

"Lovey, what's going on?" Brie asked.

"We have to find Randall!" Lovey cried.

"Calm down, Ms. Dearheart. Who's Randall?" Riggs asked.

"My grandson!"

Brie had never heard Lovey talk about her children, let alone her grandchildren. Diana and Sam had told the dance class Lovey had no family besides Duchess.

Lovey tried a locked classroom door, then ran to the next one. The door jerked open. A janitor's closet.

"Randall!" Lovey yelled. She moved a mop aside. Duchess snuffled on the floor. "Randall!"

"A missing child?" Riggs asked. "I don't think he's in here."

Brie looked around him into the surprisingly neat storage room full of cleaning supplies.

"He's fourteen. A freshman. The Showcase starts in fifteen minutes!" Lovey sounded frantic.

A voice behind them startled Brie. "What seems to be the trouble, Officer Riggs?"

Brie recognized the woman's blond curls. Officer Murdock wore civilian attire. Riggs's enthusiastic partner in fighting crime grinned. She always had an unnerving look in her blue eyes, as though arresting someone would be the frosting on her cake.

"Oh hi, Maddie. There's a missing teen," Riggs said. "We need to split up. We'll cover more ground that way."

*Maddie?* It was a cute name for such a scary woman. Brie was too nervous around her to use her first name.

"Officer Murdock, what are you doing here?" Brie asked. She suddenly realized how rude that sounded and added, "It must be your day off, I mean. You're not in uniform."

"My oldest daughter has the part of The Neighbor in *The Tell-Tale Heart, Abridged* skit. I may be a single mom, but I never miss anything my kids are doing." Murdock beamed, but she still had a slightly deranged look in her eyes. Maybe it was just the way her face looked.

Today, she had on what looked to be the fraternal twin of Papa Bear's T-shirt. Murdock's said, "Mama Bear." Brie might have thought they were a matched set, but Murdock had just said she was single.

Murdock turned to address Lovey. "Do you have a picture of the missing boy?"

Lovey blushed. "I lost my phone. But he's very distinctive. He's got jet black hair, a gray Victorian-style suit with lace cuffs, a red vest, and contour makeup that's aging him into a mature man."

"Oh, Randall Hoffman? The kid playing the lead?" Murdock asked.

Lovey nodded. "Yes, that's him."

"I know who you're talking about. Let's go, people!" Murdock clapped her big, pinkish hands together. "I'll question the witnesses." Murdock spun on one rubber heel of her laceless canvas sneakers and ran down the hallway.

"I'll check upstairs." Riggs took off.

"Then I'll go this way," Brie said. She started to go the opposite way down the hallway that Murdock had gone. Anything to get away from the unstable female officer.

Duchess sniffed the floor, then started barking.

"Wait, Brie!" Lovey exclaimed. "Come with me! I think Duchess found Randall's scent."

# 33

## ✳ Thorne ✳

*What a way to spend Valentine's Day. Tracking down a senior citizen.* Thorne supposed he had his chance for romantic holidays when he'd been married to Brie's mom. Had chances and blew them all.

A familiar-looking blond woman in a "Mama Bear" T-shirt with a grizzly on it ran on stage. Thorne couldn't make heads or tails of the chaos. Was this all part of some new experiential theater? Some artsy interpretation of what plays were meant to be?

Thorne couldn't place where he'd seen the large woman before. She yelled, "Listen, everyone! Randall Hoffman is missing! If you have information as to his whereabouts, please come backstage to make an official report."

"That kid is the star of the high school's skit," Foxglove said. "I saw his name on the poster. This sounds serious."

"Actually, it sounds like a job for a private investigator." Thorne stood.

"Hold on," Foxglove said. "You're not going anywhere without me. I'm not leaving this place until I see Lovey Dearheart. Want to fuel up? I need something to sustain me."

He opened a thin black leather briefcase that looked professional but contained only fried dough rings.

The skinny guy actually lived on donuts and didn't go anywhere without a full supply.

"How many of those do you eat in a day?" Thorne asked.

"I don't keep count. My mother makes me take multivitamins," Foxglove said, "and I haven't died yet."

Maybe donuts weren't as bad for you as everyone made them out to be. Thorne was learning a lot about the guy, and was liking him more and more by the minute.

Even though Thorne had eaten two donuts on the way to the high school, he reasoned he needed more sugar for energy to help find this missing teenager. He grabbed a strawberry-frosted. "Thanks."

"Anytime."

Thorne and Foxglove made their way backstage and approached the mama bear. She had a brood of smaller bears that looked like her circling her large form. One of them was in costume. *Mama Bear is a stage mom.* Thorne had stumbled on a new breed of woman that was surely a terrifying force to be reckoned with.

"Thorne Bramble, PI." Thorne flashed his business card. "How can I be of assistance?"

"A gumshoe, eh?" The lady put out a hand to shake Thorne's. "The name's Maddie, but you can call me Officer Murdock."

Thorne gulped and gripped Officer Murdock's meaty hand. His fingernails turned blue by the time she released his grip.

She pulled out a wet wipe from a cavernous purse that looked like it could perform double duty as a gym bag. "You've got sticky fingers Mr. Gumshoe."

*Well, I did just finish three frosted donuts.*

Thorne restrained himself from responding to Murdock's comment. *Keep it professional.* The police officer in the bear shirt aggressively interviewed the teacher who was the play director. Thorne had his pick of the other adults milling around behind the stage.

"Do you know Randall?" Thorne asked a man and a woman with a little girl. They were all dressed for a rainstorm. "I'm a private investigator. I'm here to help." The family clomped up to Thorne in rubber galoshes.

"Oh, thank goodness," the woman said. "We're getting nowhere. I'm Sally Hoffman, Randall's mother. This is my husband Harry, and this is our little girl, Chrissy."

"Nice to meet you." The girl curtsied.

"Demetrius Foxglove." He put his hand out to shake Harry and Sally's. "I'll be assisting Thorne today."

*Since when?* Though Thorne couldn't complain about the steady stream of snacks.

"Where did you last see your missing son?" Foxglove asked.

"Up here on stage," Harry said.

"My brother ran away!" the little girl cried.

"Ah," Foxglove said, tapping a finger against his chin. "Troubles at home?"

"No." Sally looked mortified. "Well, Randall was a little unhappy. He didn't tell us about being in this skit because he was afraid we wouldn't approve."

"Your son is afraid of you?" Foxglove asked.

Now it was the boy's father who bristled. Foxglove was useless as an interrogator.

Thorne elbowed Foxglove to the side. "I'll handle this. Do you think he left the premises of the high school?" Thorne asked the parents.

"His bike's still back here, so I doubt it." Sally pointed to a black bicycle that looked like something from a Tim Burton film.

"Do you happen to have his shoes?" Thorne asked. "Perhaps he left footprints I can follow. Just seeing the size of his feet should narrow things down."

The winter weather made everyone's shoes a little muddy. Despite the janitor's best efforts, the tiled floors of the school were streaked with brownish, melting slush. Whether or not Randall's shoes were clean, he'd leave tracks on the dirty floors.

"They're right here." Harry led Thorne to a set of thigh-high black studded boots that would look appropriate on the feet of Marilyn Manson or a KISS band member.

Thorne placed the soles of the wild-looking boots next to his own dress shoes. The kid's feet were close to the same size as his own.

"You all have to leave." One of the teachers assisting the performers waved his hands at the group. "The Showcase is starting. Only performers are allowed backstage."

"We were just leaving," Thorne said. "Now that we've got a great lead. Come on, Foxglove."

"He's my brother! I'm coming, too!" Chrissy stomped her foot.

"We're all coming," Sally said.

"We're right behind you, detective." Harry gave a mock salute, which didn't make any sense.

"He's no detective," Murdock piped in as Thorne, Foxglove, and the Hoffmans exited the backstage area. "He's just a PI."

# 34

# ✳ Brie ✳

Brie stayed close to Lovey's side and followed the tiny poodle to a set of stairs that descended into a darkened corridor. In the distance, cheerful music played for one of the Valentine's Showcase acts. It contrasted harshly with the dire nature of their quest.

"Yip!" Duchess seemed to be saying Randall was down there.

"These stairs are so dark," Lovey said. "Mind if I hold onto you? I don't want to take a tumble."

Brie flicked on the flashlight on her smartphone, then offered an arm to Lovey. "I'm happy to help." The elderly woman wrapped her arm through Brie's. "Randall isn't the only one who's been missing," Brie said. "Where were you, Lovey?"

*And why weren't you teaching your class so I didn't have to?*

"I was visiting my family," Lovey said. This sounded just like Barry's excuse.

"I didn't know you had family," Brie said.

"Neither did I."

A light flickered. Brie saw shadows moving, and then they were gone.

She reached into her purse for her pepper spray. It was

underneath the Valentine Riggs had given her that she hadn't opened. She pulled out the new pink canister, ready for any danger.

A small white flame that didn't appear to be attached to a candle or light source floated in a pool of darkness.

*That's strange.*

"Hold it right there!" Brie called. She really didn't want to spray anyone. In her personal experience, the stuff was awful. And she had no idea if it was flammable or not.

A shadow emerged into the light of the flame. A figure dressed in black, with her face masked. Hidden. Brie had seen her before. Three times now.

A strange, distorted voice hissed, reminding Brie of a female Batman. "It should never have come to this."

The ninja held a length of the same kind of black, silky rope she had used to tie up Brie. The flame moved revealing a second form. At the end of the rope, a young man stood, lassoed, with his arms pinned to his waist.

"Randall," the ninja said. "You cannot run and hide in the shadows from your problems. That is not the way of the ninja."

Lovey stopped in her tracks.

"Randall!" Brie whispered. *He's the missing teen.*

Lovey put a hand on Brie's shoulder. "Quiet!" Lovey whispered, "The ninja is speaking to my grandson. This is his moment."

Duchess circled Lovey's feet, her claws skittering on the floor. Lovey scooped the pink poodle up in her arms. The normally energetic pup stayed silent, as if she understood the gravity of the situation.

Brie doubted the ninja was unaware of their presence. It seemed more likely she was choosing to ignore them.

"The shadows are the shields that protect our inner light. They make us strong. But they are not to be used frivolously. You must allow your parents to see you shine."

"But what if Mom and Dad hate the skit!"

"Sometimes our greatest passions are subject to the greatest scorn," the ninja said. "Are you afraid in the shadows? Or do they make you braver?"

The ninja tossed a small black orb. It burst. The flame extinguished, and the ninja disappeared in a puff of smoke.

Duchess barked. Lovey and Brie rushed forward and untied Randall.

"The skit," Lovey said. "Randall, you have to face your fear head-on. You must get on that stage."

# 35

# * Thorne *

"The footprints go down there." Thorne pointed to some stairs that descended into darkness.

Music from the theater thrummed down the hallway. Some hip-hop-sounding tune played like a soundtrack that made Thorne feel like an action-adventure movie hero.

"I had my doubts, but you're a really excellent PI, Thorne." Foxglove gave Thorne a nod of approval.

They'd had about ten false starts, but Thorne's donut-filled gut spoke to him and led them down the correct path. *The sugar finally kicked in.*

The parents and the little girl crowded behind Thorne and Foxglove at the top of the stairs. Thorne felt around the sides of the corridor for some kind of light switch. But he didn't find anything. "The lights are probably programmed to save energy on the weekends. There's got to be a maintenance override somewhere, but we're out of time to go looking for that."

"We have to go down there? Really?" Harry looked ready to wet himself.

"Why does my brother have a dark soul, Mommy?" Chrissy's lower lip quivered.

"Oh Chrissy!" Sally bent down and folded the little girl into a hug. "Randall doesn't have a dark soul. He just has a different way of looking at things."

"Even blacklights shine," Harry said. "They just cast a different kind of light."

"Mommy! Daddy! I never thought of it that way!" Chrissy smiled from ear to ear.

The kid acted like she was five years old, but Thorne guessed she was around twice that age. Thorne grimaced when the entire family gathered in a group hug. A pang of jealousy tugged at Thorne's heart. He and Brie had never been this close.

"Be brave, Chrissy. Let's go get your brother and save his show!" Sally exclaimed.

The family high-fived each other and followed Thorne and Foxglove down the dark stairs. Thorne couldn't find the flashlight app on the remnants of his phone.

"How can you possibly pick up hotties with that busted phone?" Foxglove asked. "How do you run your PI business with that thing?"

"It's the best I can do right now," Thorne grumbled. *It's not like I can afford a new one.*

Foxglove, and everyone else, flicked on their smartphones, but it was still very dark.

Thorne flinched when he felt something brush his hand. He glanced back and saw Foxglove standing right behind him.

"Um, you mind if I . . . Um . . . I'm not into the dark." Foxglove's voice trembled.

*Must be why the womanizing guy doesn't want to sleep alone.* Although, throughout Thorne's surveillance, the only woman he observed Foxglove with in his personal life was his mother. He might have been getting social contacts from hot women, but the guy didn't seem to get any further than that. Thorne imagined Foxglove in a boy's childhood bedroom sleeping with a nightlight.

Thorne felt Foxglove's hand wrap around his own and squeeze on tight. Thorne gave a return squeeze. *Cis-het dudes have to look out for each other.*

When they reached the bottom, three dark figures approached them.

"Brie!" *When did she get here?* He jerked his hand out of Foxglove's death-grip and grabbed Brie by the shoulders. "Are you okay?"

"Hi, Dad," Brie said, taking a step back from her father.

"What happened?" Thorne asked.

"We've got everything under control." In her hand was a coil of silky black rope.

An old-looking dude in a gray suit with lacy cuffs stepped into the glow of the smartphones. "Mom, Dad. I'm sorry if you don't like it, but the show must go on."

*This is the missing kid? Teenagers these days must have rough lives.*

Randall's old-timey costume contrasted darkly with the bright yellow raincoats the rest of his family wore. The teen continued. "I love this skit. It speaks to who I am. And if it means you don't love me anymore—"

Randall didn't get to finish his sentence. The Hoffmans slammed into him like a football team tackling the guy with the ball. But in an affectionate way. They hugged, and cooed, and coddled, and Thorne felt his blood sugar rise to a dangerously high level.

"Daddy said you're a shiny blacklight," Chrissy said. "And I like blacklights because they make things glow in the dark. Just like you, Randall. I think my heart is glowing! But where's Grandma?"

The third person stepped into the glow of the smartphone lights. "Everything is sunshine and roses down here." Lovey Dearheart was wearing the biggest smile of all.

"It's Lovey! She's really here!" Foxglove jumped up and down, practically levitating. He wrung his hands together.

"Why are you hanging back, Grandma?" Randall sniffed. "Get in here!"

"Don't cry, dear," Lovey said, folding in with the others.

"You'll mess up your makeup."

"I just love a happy ending," Harry said. "We love you, Mom."

Lovey's makeup was dissolving down her cheeks. "I . . . I love you all so much!"

"Waaaaa!" Tears leaked out of Foxglove's dark brown eyes. "This is so beautiful!" He piled into the hug and stretched his long, skinny arms around the entire group.

Thorne glanced at Brie. She opened her mouth, stuck out her tongue, and made a gagging face.

*Yep. We've never been that kind of family, and maybe we never will be.*

After this went on entirely too long, Thorne clapped his hands together. "All right, everyone, wrap it up! Don't you have a performance to get to?"

"Oh, Randall, hurry!" Lovey cried.

They all raced up the stairs, leaving Thorne and Brie behind. They walked slowly toward the bright corridor. Brie was still clutching the black silky rope in one hand.

"So, what's the rope for?" Thorne asked.

"This? It's not mine." Brie said. "It's the ninja's."

# 36

# ✳ Lovey ✳

"Look at my costume. I'm a disaster!" Randall wailed backstage.

"You look just fine," Lovey tried to reassure him. Despite her warning, he'd shed tears, which had streaked the cakey white makeup on his cheeks. Lovey was skilled in touchups and had learned even more from Sam Slate. She licked the corner of her pink handkerchief and smoothed the makeup to cover the tear trails.

A troupe of tiny dancers in flouncy red tutus skittered off the stage, giggling. From the applause, Lovey guessed they'd been a big hit.

"The cameraman just told me." A woman who had the look of a teacher interrupted Lovey and Randall. She pressed a clipboard to her flat chest and waved a hand at the guy with the frizzy red man-bun standing behind a camera on a tripod. "You're Lovey Dearheart, correct?"

"That's me," Lovey replied. "The hopeless romantic."

"I'm a huge fan," the teacher gushed. "I think Randall and the other students need to calm down before the show goes on. Would you do us the honor of entertaining the audience for a few moments? Maybe give an intro for the skit?"

"Oh!" Lovey said in surprise. She wasn't prepared to speak,

but she had plenty of experience with improv. "I'd love to."

"It's live streaming on social media," the teacher said. "Will you be all right?"

"She's got this," Randall said. He gave her the biggest smile yet, nearly cracking his layers of aging makeup.

Lovey stepped onto the stage with Duchess in one arm, and a wireless microphone in her free hand. Duchess gave her an encouraging doggy kiss on her chin. Lovey took a deep breath and spoke from the heart.

"Edgar Allen Poe's *The Tell-Tale Heart* is a production usually reserved for Halloween. And certainly never Valentine's Day. Today is for lovers. People whose hearts have been pierced by Cupid's arrow, instead of pounding under the floorboards, placed there by a madman."

Lovey paused to look out into the audience. The faces all blurred into anonymity in the darkness. But Lovey knew the Hoffmans were watching. She spoke directly to them.

"My career was all about love. Every movie I introduced on my show *The Hopeless Romantic* had a happy ending. You'd get to the end and know that the characters had found their perfect love. The kind that can only exist in fictional worlds."

Lovey squeezed Duchess a little tighter, steadying herself before she continued.

"Most of the people watching my show never found that in real life. That's why they looked for it in movies. Humans crave the fulfillment of the ideal, the hearts and flowers of Valentine's Day, having faith that every real love story can have a happily ever after. But how often does it really happen that way?"

Lovey thought of the destroyed and repaired ninja contract. It would no longer accept signatures. Did this mean Lovey's own dream of true love was over? She caught Randall peeking at her from the wings. His smile made Lovey's optimism flood back into her heart.

"My name is Lovey, but I haven't been lucky in love." She grinned. "Until now."

Lovey stopped herself. She needed to wrap this up.

"Many hearts may be dark tonight on this holiday of love. The next skit is for all the folks out there who haven't found that perfect love. An anti-valentine, if you will. Love is a connection to other human hearts. Hopefully, healthier than the one in the skit coming up. And now, may I present to you, *The Tell-Tale Heart, Abridged*."

Lovey stepped off the stage as the curtain rose. She dashed to find a seat in the audience. The Hoffmans waved her over to where they were sitting. She settled beside Sally, who reached out and squeezed Lovey's hand. Lovey looked at Sally's face in the dim light. Tears glistened on the younger woman's cheeks as she mouthed what looked like the words, "That was wonderful."

Lovey's second viewing of the high school skit was even better than the first. She and Sally held hands the entire time. Just like a mother and daughter should.

When the skit was over, *The Tell-Tale Heart, Abridged* received a standing ovation. Randall's parents cheered loudest of all, even drowning out Lovey's cries of "Bravo!"

The Hoffmans stayed standing.

"We need to get ready for our performance," Harry said.

Lovey followed the Hoffmans backstage.

# 37

# ❋ Brie ❋

*That was pretty creepy for a Valentine's Day skit.* But Brie had never had a "real" Valentine's Day. *What do I know?*

"That Randall kid was incredible," Dad said.

"He's got star power." Demetrius Foxglove nodded with approval.

"Yeah. Randall was amazing," Brie agreed.

It was time well spent watching the teenager in action. Foxglove looked vaguely familiar to Brie. She didn't have time to puzzle it out right now.

After the skit, Brie went backstage to find the HMCA seniors. To wish them luck, or that their legs got broken or something.

"Lovey!" Brie heard several voices exclaim.

Ramona, Poppy, and the senior dance class clustered around Lovey Dearheart. Professor Fluffingston circled Lovey's legs, looking up at Duchess in her arms. The seniors' sequined costumes sparkled under the lighting. Feather boas flounced. Some of the women cooled themselves, waving ostrich plume fans. *Hot flashes? Or just pre-performance jitters.* They looked excited. Ready. Brie could only hope they didn't bomb onstage.

"How was the romance convention?" Diana Diamond asked Lovey, with one eyebrow raised.

"Oh! Actually, I had a family emergency," Lovey said, hugging Duchess tightly in her arms. "I'm sorry I couldn't be there for you all."

George said, "Well, you could have found a real sub instead of sticking us with this stoner." He jabbed a finger in Brie's direction.

"Brie taught my class? I didn't know you could dance, dear," Lovey said.

Before Brie could speak for herself, the entire class shouted, "She can't!"

"That charming young police officer is the one who actually taught while you were away, Lovey," the cookie lady said.

"Where is Riggs?" Diana asked. "We're going on after the next act."

"Right here," Riggs stepped up to the group. "You don't need me anymore. You guys have mastered this dance. Besides, I'm not dressed for this." He patted the bulky service belt strapped around his narrow hips. The man looked incredible in uniform. "I'm on duty, and I have some questions for Ms. Dearheart." He turned to Lovey. "I heard you say you had a family emergency. Is everything all right?"

Lovey smiled. "I'm almost certain it is. Thank you for helping out while I was away."

Ramona piped in, "Brie tried her best to help."

"If Professor Fluffingston hadn't been so opposed to the style of dance you chose, I would have helped out, too," Poppy offered.

"I'm just glad you could meet us here to watch the show, Poppy," Ramona said. "The entire Showcase has been a real treat."

"Too bad you couldn't ride in the van with us," Layton said.

"It was for the best. The Professor prefers quieter vehicles."

Brie moved away from the group. Her annoying father joined her.

"That's the coolest cat in town." Dad made moon-eyes at

the Professor.

"If he's so sensitive, how the heck can he handle a theater full of people?" Brie asked.

"That's a good point. He seems calm enough. Cats are amazing creatures. Look! They can sleep through anything!"

The cat curled up near Poppy's feet and closed his eyes.

*Sheesh!* Brie's mind whirred as people chatted. "Ramona drove the Hummingbird Gardens transport van again. Poppy came separately. If she's the ninja, that would have given her time to come early and change in and out of ninja gear."

Dad held his hands out palms up like he was exasperated. "There you go with that ninja stuff again. What would Poppy have done with Professor Fluffingston? Did you see a cat where you found Randall?"

"No, but maybe the cat isn't really an alibi. What if Poppy is only pretending to be obsessed with him? If that's the case, she could have totally left him in her car while she did ninja stuff."

"Yeah, but have you met the Professor. How could you not be obsessed with that guy?"

*Maybe Dad's not the most skilled private investigator. After all, he does work for peanut brittle.*

Dad continued, "What about that No Boys Allowed Club you told me about. Did you know Diana is incredibly fast at picking locks?"

"Um, yeah. She's a retired locksmith according to her HMCA paperwork. But why do you know about that?"

"No reason," Dad said, looking away.

"Sam and the cookie lady were here the whole time, too. Any one of them could have slipped away unnoticed while we were searching for Randall."

"But Sam isn't shaped like a woman." Thorne lifted his fedora slightly and scratched his head. "Or a man either, come to think of it."

Brie considered Sam's room full of costuming supplies.

"Sam can look however they want," Brie replied.

"You really think one of these retirees is your ninja?" he asked with a smirk.

"Why not?"

Dad looked skeptical.

Brie threw her hands up in frustration. "You still don't believe me! Whatever! There really is a ninja, Dad." She walked away from him in a huff.

The seniors must have moved offstage to prepare for their performance. Only Lovey and her family huddled backstage in silence. Brie joined them. The sound of applause heralded the end of the current act.

Lovey's granddaughter said, "We're next, Grandma."

"I'll be watching from the wings," Lovey said.

Brie followed Lovey and Duchess to a place behind the curtain off to the side of the stage. She had questions for Lovey.

The woman was all alone in the world. That's what everyone thought. Until this week. A week during which Brie had once again seen the shapely female ninja.

Brie knew she wasn't crazy. Even if several people in her life thought otherwise. Brie reached out to pat the curly pink crown of fur on Duchess's little head. Something was definitely missing.

Brie reached into her purse and pulled out the red rosette collar decoration from her box of girly stuff. She handed it to Lovey. "I think this belongs to Duchess."

"Oh my!" Lovey clipped the rosette to the toy poodle's collar. "Where did you find this?"

"Here at the theater on Tuesday night," Brie said. "You were here with the Hoffmans, weren't you."

The blush on Lovey's cheeks deepened in color.

"Why didn't you let the dance class know you were all right?"

"It's complicated," Lovey hedged. "Watch out!"

Stagehands hurried through with a backdrop and props for

the Hoffmans.

"They're setting up the stage for my family's routine," Lovey said.

"Everyone was so worried about you," Brie said in a stage whisper. "We all have been."

Brie had hoped her comments would prompt Lovey to give some explanation for her nearly week-long absence. Instead, the senior placed a hand on Brie's forearm and gave a gentle squeeze.

"I was a little worried myself," she told Brie. "But worry is a wasted emotion."

"Was the ninja involved in your disappearance?" Brie asked. Lovey couldn't deny the mysterious woman's existence like everyone else. Brie and Lovey had both witnessed the ninja with Randall.

"I was hoping to see her again after she helped my grandson. But you know how ninjas are," Lovey said.

"I'm starting to." Brie studied Lovey's face, but got no more answers.

"Oh look!" Lovey exclaimed in a hushed voice. "Quiet. My family is starting."

Brie watched a fanciful performance of the main song from *Singin' in the Rain* turn stormy when that talented Randall kid broke up the action with an intense rendition of "Send in the Clowns." Brie went from elation to tears, and back again, when the family ended on a happy note.

As the curtain closed and the Hoffman family went off stage, the HMCA senior dance class began to line up for their performance. Brie needed to return to the audience to really see the dance.

She spun around on her heel and almost ran into Riggs.

"Eeek!"

He pulled his hands up to his chest in a defensive posture. "Sorry! I didn't mean to startle you."

"It's okay. I'm just a little on edge from all the excitement."

*And I thought you might be a ninja.*

"That's all over, hopefully," Riggs said. "I'm done questioning people. I need to get back on patrol."

"Aren't you gonna watch your grandpa? He's going on now! It's only like a minute long."

Riggs smiled. "I guess I can spare a minute."

"Come on. Let's go find seats."

Brie sat next to Riggs. It was almost like being on a real date.

The seniors did a great job, bumping and grinding with their feather boas. They looked ready to take flight as their ostrich feather plume fans flapped wildly. Even George was smiling. Layton Lambert finished the number by dropping into the splits. The crowd went wild.

The seniors were the last act in the showcase. When the lights came up and people began dispersing, Riggs turned to Brie.

"That was cool," Riggs said. "I really do have to go now. My shift doesn't end until midnight. Maybe Officer Murdock can give you a ride home."

*Murdock! She'd probably drive me directly to the Criminal Justice Center, just because.* Brie glimpsed a waving hand. *Dad!* He had finally taken off the dog print-coated brown winter trench coat, but his black leather overcoat still stood out in a crowd. *And he almost never takes that stupid hat off.*

"I'll catch a ride with my father." Brie hoped that wasn't a look of relief on the police officer's face. But she was afraid it might be.

He turned to leave, but spun back around. "Hey, did you get a chance to look at my card?"

Brie reached into her purse for the card Riggs gave her that morning. She pulled out the big red envelope. Lifted the flap. Removed the card.

*No hearts, arrows, or cupids.*

Printed on the front in red was "Happy Valentine's Day to

a Nice Person." Inside it read, "I'm Glad We're Friends."

*It's official. We're in the friend zone.*

Brie didn't know why she expected anything more. The cookie lady had claimed that eating her Valentine's treats would guarantee love on the holiday. *Why should I believe in a silly cookie?*

Gaining a new friend in her mostly solitary life was pretty sweet. And wasn't yesterday called Galentine's? A holiday for women, celebrating female friendship. *Not that I have any female friends, either.* Maybe Riggs was her Pal-entine. It wasn't the romantic version of love she expected the magic cookie to bring. *And face it, the "date" could have been romantic if I wasn't a total dweeb.*

*So maybe the cookies work, after all.*

"This is a nice card!" she told Riggs. "I'm glad we're friends, too."

"Okay, well." He gave a little wave with one hand. "Catch you later."

This definitely hadn't been Brie's best Valentine's Day. She thought for a moment, watching the handsome police officer leave. Not the worst, either.

*Yeah, definitely not the worst.*

# 38

# ❋ Lovey ❋

"Come on, Grandma. We're going out to get heart-shaped pizza from Louie's Pizzeria to celebrate."

Chrissy and Duchess pranced around Lovey in circles in the high school hall. Only a few cast members and families were still milling around.

"Did you like the Showcase, Mom?" Harry asked.

"I loved it! This has been the best Valentine's Day of my life," Lovey gushed. "And that's saying a lot, considering how many of the holidays I've lived to see."

"Randy, er, um, Randall," Harry said. "That was amazing. I've been a darned fool."

"You're incredible," Sally said.

"My brother was fan-tas-tic!" Chrissy locked her arms around Randall.

He returned the hug. "Wow, thanks, guys! I should have told you the truth from the start."

Harry and Sally joined in the hug.

"Get in here!" Harry waved Lovey over.

Group hugs seemed to be a frequent happening with this family. She piled in.

"Thank you, Grandma," Randall said.

"We all owe you thanks," Harry said. "I feel like I lost my

mind. What was I thinking? I really do need a mom. You helped us see Randall for who he really is."

Sally said, "He might not be exactly like the rest of us, but that's what makes him special. We got so caught up in what we thought Valentine's Day was supposed to look like that we forgot about the most important part."

"The love!" Chrissy exclaimed. Everyone hugged each other a little tighter. "Wait a minute! Grandma's not official yet!" She snatched the roll of parchment from her mother's purse and handed it to her father. Then she carefully pulled out the raven feather pen and pot of ink.

"Do you think it will work now?" Sally asked?

"What do you mean?" Randall asked.

"Daddy and Grandma tried to sign it this morning," Chrissy said, "but the ink wouldn't stick."

Everyone held their breath as Lovey took the quill in her quaking fingers. She dipped it into the ink pot.

Lovey glanced around at the people she wanted so badly to call her family, hesitating before touching the tip of the quill to the contract.

"It's working! It's working!" Chrissy bounced on her toes.

A rich, black dot melded into the rice paper parchment with permanence. As Lovey drew the quill across the contract, adding her signature, she felt so happy she could burst. She always made the "o" in her name into a heart, and took special care to inscribe it with perfection.

The rest of the family carefully added their signatures.

"You've all been so wonderful," Lovey said, fighting back tears.

"Excuse me, Ms. Dearheart?" The man-bun camera guy rushed up to Lovey with Demetrius Foxglove in tow. "This is the person I was telling you about. He'd love an autograph."

Foxglove shoved a Valentine's Showcase program and a pen toward Lovey.

*Oh no, not him.* He had been spamming Lovey with snail

and e-mail for weeks. Lovey didn't want to be a part of his womanizing podcast. He had terrible ideas about love.

"I know all about this man," Lovey said. "I'll give you my autograph, but after this, you need to leave me alone."

Lovey signed Foxglove's program.

"Can I get your signature, too, young man?" Foxglove addressed Randall. "You're going places!"

"And I'm going places, too," Lovey said. "Home with my family."

"Wait," Demetrius Foxglove choked out. He was in tears again. "I'm a huge fan! I used to watch your romance movie show when I was a little boy with my mommy," sniff sniff, "and I just," sniff, "want," sniff sniff—

"He wants to interview you on his show." Thorne Bramble stepped up to the group with his daughter, Brie.

Duchess leapt down from Lovey's arms and greeted Thorne like he was an old friend. *Funny, I don't think they've ever met.*

"Hey, I've seen you on my socials," Randall said, pointing toward Foxglove. "And I have something to say about The Love Parlor."

"Spill the tea, young man," Lovey said, testing out more of Randall's teen slang.

"Your stupid show sucks!" Randall exclaimed.

"Randall, language!" Sally said.

"It's true. But I think you should do his show, Grandma," Randall said. "He needs help."

"He's not that bad," Thorne said.

Foxglove got down on his knees and wrung his hands. "Please, Ms. Dearheart? I agree that my show could be better, but I'm actually working on a new channel. Branching out. I've landed a generous sponsor desperate for content. When I saw you all on stage, I realized you have what my brand is missing: family."

"Get up! You're ruining that nice suit," Lovey told Foxglove.

He stood up and dusted himself off, towering over Lovey.

Lovey asked, "What are you talking about?"

"I've written scripts for a series of shorts that your family will be perfect for. They're full of singing, dancing, and always include a valuable lesson."

"We have day jobs," Sally said. "A family to support."

"But I can pay all of you!" Foxglove said.

"What should we do, Mom?" Harry asked.

Lovey looked around at her new family. This was precisely the kind of opportunity the Hoffmans had been dreaming of all of their lives.

"I think you know what I would have done," Lovey said. "You need to pursue your dreams."

Foxglove took Lovey's hands in his own. "My receptionist will be in touch to get everything set up!"

He ran off and joined his cameraman, who was putting away his equipment from livestreaming and recording the Valentine's Showcase.

Before she could leave, the PI stepped in front of her.

"Lovey, I have some questions for you," Thorne said.

"Well, I guess you can have my number if you really want it," Lovey replied, batting her eyes. She loved watching him turn beet red.

"Um, I . . ." Thorne swallowed. "Where have you been all week?"

"I was with my family," Lovey said with a smile. "I suppose I should put my cottage up for rent."

"We'll make all those arrangements on Monday," Harry said. "In the meantime, we'd better hurry if we're going to get that heart-shaped pizza for dinner!"

Randall and Chrissy both cheered. Lovey threw her arms around her grandchildren.

*So this is how my happily ever after begins.*

# 39

# ❋ Thorne ❋

**Thorne was relieved** that Foxglove got a ride with Lance, the camera dude. Brie needed a ride home, and while he liked Foxglove as a man's man, he was too dangerous to have around his inexperienced daughter.

"Can you believe Harry met Sally and had a couple of kids? How funny is that?" Brie asked.

"You knew those people already?" Thorne asked.

"No. Remember Mom's favorite movie? She must have watched it a thousand times."

"Oh, that," Thorne said. But he really didn't remember. *I was probably drunk or at work whenever she watched it,* he thought with disgust. That must have been pretty lonely for her. No wonder she ran away to Tibet.

**The ride settled** into silence. Thorne wasn't sure whether Brie was exhausted from all the excitement or if she just didn't want to talk to her old dad. She held the weird black rope in her lap, running her fingers over it.

"That rope," Thorne said. "You said it belongs to that ninja lady?"

"She keeps showing up," Brie said. "She also left this at my house when she got Duchess." Brie pulled a hard plastic case from her purse and produced a small, ornate ninja knife.

When Thorne pulled to a stop at a red light, he picked up the knife and examined it. "This is amazing. And it looks sharp enough to shave with." Thorne held it near his stubble-covered cheek.

"Dad! Give me that!" Brie reached for the knife. "And pay attention. The light just changed."

Thorne handed the blade to Brie. She tucked it back into a purple plastic box in her purse.

"Be careful with that thing," Thorne said. He glanced at the box. Why was she keeping it with her girly stuff? Thorne tried not to be grossed out. It was a natural part of a young woman's life, after all. And the items did provide padding for the sharp blade.

"*You're* telling *me* to be careful?" Brie snapped. "I remember you used to shave while you were driving the car all the time. You don't still do that, do you?"

Thorne blushed and changed the subject. "So what do you know about this ninja person?"

"She has to have something to do with seniors going missing."

"Barry and Lovey told us they were just spending time with their families."

"Two families they had never mentioned to anyone before?" Brie asked skeptically. "I work next to Hummingbird Gardens. Most of the residents belong to the HMCA. So I hear their stories all the time. Senior citizens love talking about their kids and grandkids, at least when they have good relationships with them. Even the troubled families share too much information about their deadbeat offspring."

"You mean like Marty?" Thorne asked.

"He's not that bad," Brie said.

Thorne gripped the steering wheel tighter. He knew things about Marty that his innocent daughter didn't.

"Barry and Lovey have the sweetest families I've ever seen," Brie continued. "Which makes it seem peculiar that they didn't brag about these people. But think about it, Dad. There is one thread connecting the two disappearances: the ninja."

"Supposing for the sake of argument there's something to it," Thorne said. "What is this ninja's endgame?"

"However the ninja is involved, I think she has good intentions."

*Another family pieced back together, and this whole situation has ninja clues written all over it.*

Thorne's gut rumbled. He pulled a piece of lint-covered peanut brittle out of his overcoat pocket and nibbled sullenly.

"Want some?" He held out a piece for Brie.

"Gross! What even is that?"

"The cookie lady's peanut brittle."

"Is it moldy?" Brie asked, making a disgusted face.

"It's just a little pocket lint. My coat was clean when I put it in there. Here."

"No thanks."

"Fine. More for me!" Thorne tossed the rest of the piece in his mouth. The lint added an interesting texture that wasn't half bad. And his doctor told him he needed more fiber in his diet.

The conversation stalled out as they neared Brie's neighborhood. His ex-wife's house. Where he used to live. Thorne wasn't ready to end the night. His New Year's resolution to be a better father wasn't progressing the way he hoped. He had so much more to say to his daughter. But he didn't even know how to begin.

He felt like a failure, and it stung. To make matters worse, he wasn't the one to find Lovey. Lance, the camera guy did. *What kind of a pathetic PI am I?*

The good news was that Lovey said she'd be returning to work tomorrow. The bad news was, Thorne could have been doing a real job for real money all this time, and nothing much would have changed.

But Thorne had a gut feeling that there was more to this situation than met the eye. Brie acted innocently enough. *But come on!* That black rope. The kunai knife.

Brie claimed she found them. But what if they were really hers? Did she become a ninja while he was skimping on his parental duties? She had brought up several people that could potentially be the ninja. Were her theories misdirection? The whole thing sounded insane.

The peanut brittle sat heavily in Thorne's gut, on top of all the donuts Foxglove had fed him. He wondered what Foxglove had planned for tonight. Was he dining in his castle with one of his many princesses? Thorne snorted. *More likely he's having donuts and bad coffee with his mom.*

All these thoughts about food caused Thorne's stomach to rumble with hunger. He needed a real meal. Thorne glanced at his daughter.

"Want to grab a bite to eat?" he asked with trepidation. He was certain he'd be rejected.

Brie was silent for a moment, then glanced at him. "All I've eaten today was a bubble tea. What did you have in mind?"

It was Valentine's night. Every nice restaurant in town would be packed with romantic diners. *I have my own real princess, and I know just the castle I can take her to.*

"Let's go to King's Chef Diner," Thorne suggested.

"That place that looks like a tiny castle?" Brie scrunched up her cute little nose. Then she smiled. "Sure, Dad. You can be my Valentine."

Thorne breathed a sigh of relief. And happiness. This would be the first Valentine's Day in many years that he didn't spend alone. *If I had taken a paid job, things wouldn't have turned out this way.*

"I'll look up how to get there," Thorne said.

Chandos's base trim level didn't include the built-in GPS option. Thorne pulled over and took out his phone to navigate.

"Yikes! What is that?" Brie leaned away from Thorne.

"My phone. I dropped it." *Multiple times.*

"Don't touch it! You'll cut yourself." Brie handed Thorne

her phone. "Use mine."

He fumbled with the touchscreen and accidentally opened her photo gallery. He noticed a selfie she had taken of herself and Marty.

*Baby's first date.* He surreptitiously sent it to himself. *She'll thank me later.*

"You're taking too long," Brie said.

Thorne closed the app just as Brie snatched the phone from him.

"Let me navigate," she said.

A few taps later, and they were on their way to the castle.

*Just me and my little girl.* This was going to be the best Valentine's "date" ever.

The End

# True Love Cookies

Yields: 2 dozen cookies, although it depends on the size of the cookie cutters you're using

Note: Gluten gives some people tummy aches, but everyone should have a little love in their lives. Consider baking the gluten-free option when making them for a crowd.

## Cookie Dough

In a bowl with a hand mixer, or in a stand mixer combine:

- 3/4 cup (1 1/2 sticks) unsalted butter, softened
- 1 cup white sugar
- 1/2 teaspoon sea salt
- 1/2 teaspoon cream of tartar
- 1 teaspoon baking powder

Add in:

- 1 teaspoon vanilla extract
- 1/2 teaspoon almond extract
- 2 eggs

Mix well before adding:

- 2 1/2 cups gluten-free flour
- 1/4 cup almond flour
- Or
- 2 1/2 cups all-purpose flour
- Plus additional flour for dusting

Mix for about a minute, or until mixture forms a smooth ball of dough.

Transfer dough into an airtight container. Chill in the refrigerator for at least an hour. Be patient. Your rolling pin will thank you later.

## Assembly

Preheat oven to 350° F and line a large baking sheet with parchment paper.

Place chilled dough on a lightly floured surface and roll to about 1/4-inch thickness. Thicker rolling will make softer cookies. Thinner will make them crisp. But too thin and they'll be like crackers instead of cookies! Cut with heart-shaped cookie cutters.

Place on prepared baking sheet, and top with a dusting of pink and red Valentines sprinkles.

Bake for 8-10 minutes, or until bottoms and edges turn light brown.

Cool on wire rack before serving.

## Instructions for use:

Eat one cookie with love in your heart. The cookies will attract someone special into your life.

— The Cookie Lady, Hummingbird Gardens Senior Apartments

# Acknowledgements

We're grateful to know many fascinating people who live with the courage to pursue their dreams, like our fictional character Lovey Dearheart. Believing in yourself can be challenging in a world that too often values material achievement over artistic expression. Unfortunately, family doesn't always support our dreams. Sometimes we have to find our family of the heart to give us the encouragement to continue, especially when success seems far away.

Some brave souls make it their life's mission to help other people achieve their dreams. Thank you to good role models like the Colorado Springs dance instructors at Barbara Ellis Studio of Dance, and Best of Ballroom. Merida would like to give special thanks to Jessica Mancini, who has spent several years patiently teaching her and her husband how not to embarrass themselves ballroom dancing in public.

Humor is what gets us through the difficulties in life. Our books are meant to entertain and hopefully be a fun escape for our readers during stressful times. We hope these stories are silly and poignant in equal measures.

Thank you to all the readers who leave reviews of our work. Even just a few short words are more helpful than you know.

And as always, we thank our ever-supportive husbands, children, and our furry and finned friends. None of this would be possible without them.

# About the Mother-Daughter Writing Team

Catherine Dilts is the author of twelve novels. Her short stories appear regularly in Alfred Hitchcock's Mystery Magazine. Most of her published works have a cozy mystery flavor. After a career in environmental compliance for a global corporation, Catherine now writes fiction full time.

Catherine has completed two marathons and two ultramarathons. She enjoys spending time in the mountains and out in nature. She shares her life with her wonderful husband, two daughters, three granddaughters, puppy, three grandcats, and one granddog. You can find Catherine on her website at www.catherinedilts.com, on Facebook @catherinediltsauthor and on Instagram @diltscathy.

Merida Bass taught mathematics at the college level before pursuing her artistic dreams. When she isn't working on the novels she co-authors with her mother, Merida writes and illustrates children's books, and creates massive pencil and ink artwork measured in feet, not inches. Her YouTube channel features videos of her actively drawing, and her blog follows her training for and participation in extreme endurance events.

Merida, her husband, and three children, love international travel, camping and hiking through America's National Parks, and dressing in homemade costumes for cosplay at anime and science fiction conventions. Merida can be found at www.merida-creates.com, and on YouTube, Instagram, and Facebook with @meridacreates.